Contents

6 CHELSEA WALK, 1764

Basement

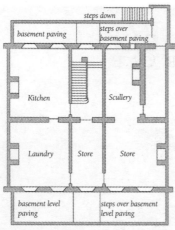

steps down

basement paving

steps over basement paving

Kitchen

Scullery

Laundry

Store

Store

basement level paving

steps over basement level paving

Ground-floor

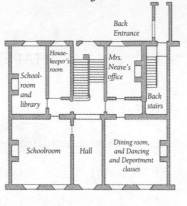

Back Entrance

School-room and library

House-keeper's room

Mrs. Neave's office

Back stairs

Schoolroom

Hall

Dining room, and Dancing and Deportment classes

First-floor

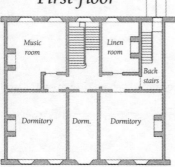

Music room

Linen room

Back stairs

Dormitory

Dorm.

Dormitory

Second-floor

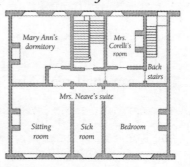

Mary Ann's dormitory

Mrs. Corelli's room

Back stairs

Mrs. Neave's suite

Sitting room

Sick room

Bedroom

Roof space

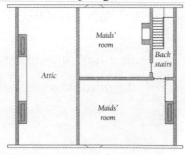

Maids' room

Back stairs

Attic

Maids' room

CHAPTER ONE

A New School

Mary Ann had read Mrs. Neave's advertisement card so many times, and with such happy anticipation, that she knew it by heart:

MRS. NEAVE'S BOARDING SCHOOL
FOR YOUNG LADIES

*A genteel riverside establishment in the village of
Chelsea, having the advantage of clean air and*

proximity to the countryside, and yet within four miles
of the City. Parents may be assured that every care is
taken of our pupils, and attention paid to their manners
and behaviour at all times. Young ladies are taught:
English, French, Arithmetic, Geography, Needlework,
Deportment and Dancing; with the opportunity to take
lessons in Singing and Harpsichord at a small extra cost.
21 guineas a year.

Singing and harpsichord lessons! Mary Ann could imagine nothing she would like more. And that small extra cost would easily be borne by her father, who spared no expense if it would further his children's advancement in the world. Her mother had visited Mrs. Neave's establishment and pronounced it suitable, and today, 30th April 1764, Mary Ann was to leave home.

She looked out of the window and glimpsed, between rooftops and chimneys, the Thames, busy with small boats. Soon she would be there, on the river, on her way to Chelsea. Now that the moment had come she felt a rush of affection for her home, for her family and servants, the old dog Bullet with his unsteady waddle and adoring eyes, the familiar streets of the City.

Her elder sister Harriet tapped at the door and came in.

"I see you are dressed and ready." She joined Mary Ann at the window. "Are you nervous?"

"Yes." It would be strange to be away from home, sharing every moment with other girls. And what would those girls be like? Most of them would be older than her: "refined, elegant young ladies", Mrs. Neave had told her mother. "Will they all be very grand, do you think?"

"Of course not! They'll be girls like you. You'll soon make friends."

Harriet smiled. She smiled often these days. Her own schooldays were behind her and she had recently become engaged to be married. Mary Ann thought her fiancé, Mr. Philip Browne, rather old and dull, but she supposed Harriet must like him; certainly Harriet liked the prospect of having a home and servants of her own.

"We'll write to each other," said Harriet.

"Yes! And I'll write to George."

Her brother was at a boarding school in Hertfordshire. They were close in age and she missed him.

"Mary Ann!"

Her mother's voice sounded from the floor below; and Amy, their lady's maid, came back into the room to check Mary Ann's dress and hair before allowing her downstairs to be inspected.

The sisters went down together to the drawing room, where their mother was waiting.

"Oh!" she exclaimed. "How grown-up you look, Mary Ann!"

Mary Ann's fair hair was drawn back from her face and arranged in neat curls. Her blue cotton gown (expensive but not showy, as befitted a merchant's schoolgirl daughter) was worn over a hooped frame, and this, together with stays boned at front and back, forced her to stand up straight under her mother's scrutiny.

Her mother turned her around and nodded approval. "Yes. You'll do well. And now we must go. Tom is waiting downstairs with your trunk."

They all went out into the courtyard. The servants – Sarah and Betty – came out to wish Mary Ann well, and Harriet kissed her goodbye. Bullet wagged his tail and pushed a damp nose against her hand. Her father, who went early to the coffee house to do business, had already said his farewell. Now their serving man Tom lifted the trunk and the three of them set off on the short walk to the landing stage at Old Swan Stairs.

Tom soon found them a boatman, and helped both mother and daughter aboard. The boat rocked alarmingly as Mary Ann stepped in, and it was no easy task to arrange her hooped skirts around herself as she sat down. She knew that getting in and out of boats and carriages gracefully was one of the many skills she would be expected to learn at Mrs. Neave's school.

She pulled her wrap around her shoulders as the boat moved out into the centre of the river. They left the City and travelled west, passing Whitehall, Westminster and the Houses of Parliament. Then came a great bend in the river, the buildings on the shore were less densely packed and she began to see fields beyond them. Mary Ann thought they must be nearly there, but it still seemed an age before the boatman pulled in at a small landing stage on a tree-lined bank, and she saw beyond it a road with a row of tall terraced houses facing the river.

"There is Chelsea Walk," said her mother.

They disembarked and climbed the shallow steps to the road, Tom following with the trunk.

Mrs. Neave's establishment was at Number Six: a large five-storey house of red brick with tall wrought-iron gates.

Mary Ann looked up. She had an impression of many rows of windows, all watching her as she shook down the crumpled layers of her skirts and began to pick her way across the muddy road. Beyond the gates was a short garden and a flight of steps leading to the front door.

Her mother took her hand and squeezed it. She led Mary Ann in through the gateway and up the steps, and knocked at the door. A maid – a dark-eyed, handsome girl – let them into the hall and then went to fetch her mistress.

Mary Ann stood on the black and white tiled floor and looked around at the lofty space. The hall was panelled in wood, and there were several closed doors – one with a murmur of voices behind it – and an archway leading to the back where a great staircase with polished wooden boards led up to a tall window on the half landing, then turned and carried on upwards. She felt very small.

"Mrs. Giffard!"

"Mrs. Neave."

A woman of about her mother's age had appeared. She was dressed in dark blue silk and looked, Mary Ann thought, rather severe compared to Mama in her striped yellow gown and little tilted straw hat. The two women nodded politely to each other.

"And Mary Ann," said Mrs. Neave, turning to her. "Welcome to our school."

Mary Ann made a small, nervous curtsy.

"You will take tea, Mrs. Giffard, before you return to the City?"

Her mother accepted, and Mrs. Neave called to the maid. "Tea, Jenny, in my office. And tell Mrs. Giffard's man to take the young lady's trunk to the rear entrance."

Jenny disappeared into the back area of the building.

Nearby, in the hall, a door opened and several girls of about Mary Ann's own age came out, carrying books. Mrs. Neave stopped one of them – a friendly-looking girl with auburn curls.

"Sophia, this is Mary Ann Giffard. Mary Ann, Sophia Hammond."

The girls nodded to each other, and Mary Ann felt Sophia's eyes taking in every detail of her appearance.

"Sophia will take you around the school and show you where you are to sleep. But first: say goodbye to your mother."

Mary Ann turned to her mother. She wished they did not have to say goodbye so publicly. Her mother's eyes were pink, as if she was holding back tears, and Mary Ann felt her own eyes pricking. She submitted to a brief kiss, then stepped brusquely away.

"You'll be home for Whitsun," her mother said, as if to reassure herself. "Now, be sure I hear well of you. And write to us…"

"I will," said Mary Ann, retreating, aware that Sophia was observing the exchange with interest.

When the other girl moved away Mary Ann was glad to follow her and leave the two women to discuss finance over their tea.

Sophia waved a hand at the room she had just left, and from which people were still coming out.

"The downstairs rooms are the main classrooms, and the dining room is here too." She briefly opened a door across the hall, and Mary Ann saw two long tables. "That room at the back is the office, where your mother is taking tea. Let's go upstairs. I'll show you the music room."

"Oh!" exclaimed Mary Ann. "A music room!"

"Do you like music?"

"I do. It's quite my favourite occupation. I'm to have harpsichord and singing lessons."

Sophia looked pleased. "I have music lessons too. Mrs. Corelli is our singing teacher and Mr. Ashton teaches harpsichord."

She walked ahead of Mary Ann around the turn of the grand staircase, and Mary Ann thought what a big house this was, though rather dark and old-fashioned with its unpainted wood panelling.

"Most of the rooms on this floor are dormitories

for the older girls," said Sophia. "But over here is the music room."

No one was in the room, so they were able to look around. There were shelves of books, music stands, flutes and other wind instruments, and a harpsichord.

"Do you have an instrument at home?" asked Sophia.

"A virginal. There is no space for anything bigger. But my sister and I both play."

"Sometimes Mr. Ashton plays for us," said Sophia. "He is a wonderful musician – and quite *divinely* handsome. Half the older girls are in love with him." She sighed theatrically. "But he's married, and quite old: twenty-eight at least."

"My sister's fiancé is twenty-eight," said Mary Ann.

"Oh! Your sister is getting married! When?"

"Next year, or the one after."

"And is she greatly in love?"

Mary Ann frowned. "I don't think so. But Mother says love is not to be recommended and that girls may do better without it."

"I shall insist on being in love when *I* marry," said Sophia.

"I don't think I want to marry at all," said Mary Ann.

Sophia's eyes opened wide. "But you would not wish to be a spinster?"

"I want to be a singer – at the opera." Mary Ann did not often tell anyone this, for it was difficult to convey how strongly she wished it, but Sophia seemed to invite confidences. She added, "Of course my parents say it is not a respectable profession."

"But you might catch the attention of a lord – and marry him! Several famous singers have. Think of that!"

She went on to ask Mary Ann about her family, and to talk about her own: her two younger brothers and baby sister; their house in Holborn; their spaniel.

"Come upstairs," she said. "I'll show you our room. Your trunk should be there by now."

They went up yet another flight to another panelled hall full of closed doors.

"Those rooms at the front are Mrs. Neave's own apartment," said Sophia, "and Mrs. Corelli has this room by the stairs. Our dormitory is here. It's above the music room."

She opened the door into a plain room with four beds, neatly made, a few chairs, and a washstand with jug, bowl and mirror. Mary Ann's trunk was standing in front of the fireplace.

"Your clothes go in that cupboard by the door," said Sophia. She eyed the trunk, and Mary Ann knew she wanted to be there when it was opened.

She saw that the bed in the far corner seemed to be hers; the others had chairs or shelves with small things – a prayer book, a handkerchief, a locket – on them.

"Who else sleeps here?" she asked.

"Lucy Stanley, over there." Sophia indicated a bed set a little separate from the others, in the space behind the door. "And Phoebe Merrill, here, next to me. You may have the corner bed. We are the youngest girls in the school. Lucy and I are thirteen; we have been here since January. And Phoebe is twelve. She came a few weeks ago. How old are you?"

"Twelve," said Mary Ann. "Thirteen in September."

Sophia smiled. "We shall all be great friends, I'm sure. Phoebe – well, everyone likes Phoebe. And Lucy is our clever one; we are quite in awe of her." She glanced again at Mary Ann's trunk. "You should unpack soon or your clothes will be creased. I'll show you where they go."

She opened a cupboard beside the door, revealing shelves and a few hooks for hanging clothes. Most of the space was taken up by full-skirted gowns and petticoats.

"There are two hooks here," said Sophia, "and these lower shelves. Cloaks and hats go in the other cupboard. Have you brought much?"

"No."

Mary Ann lifted the lid of the trunk. Her night chemise lay on top and she removed it and laid it on her bed. Sophia watched as she took out two cotton gowns, several chemises, stays, and a gown of pale green silk with a yellow under-skirt – "for occasions," she explained, wondering if there would be any.

Sophia stroked the silk admiringly and found a place for it in the cupboard. "You might wear that if we go to Ranelagh Gardens," she said.

"Ranelagh? To the Pleasure Gardens?" Mary Ann could scarcely believe she might go *there*. She had heard all about Chelsea's famous Ranelagh Gardens, where concerts were held on summer evenings in the Rotunda – "with a roof, so that it may be used even in bad weather", her sister had said – and where the gentry came to mingle and be seen.

"Mrs. Neave likes to take some of her girls to a concert there each summer," said Sophia.

"Oh! I should *so* love to go! Have you ever been there?"

"No. But the older girls tell me it is not to be missed."

From far below came the sound of someone ringing a bell.

"Dinner!" said Sophia. "Also not to be missed. Come and meet the others."

Chapter Two

Nymphs and Shepherds

The dining room was full of voices, movement, rustling skirts. Mary Ann felt eyes on her: the eyes of the teachers who had taken their places at the ends of each table, and those of passing girls. She felt nervous, and was glad of Sophia's presence.

"Stand here," said Sophia, "next to me."

They were at the lower table, nearest the door and the kitchen entrance. A teacher stood at the end, and opposite Mary Ann and Sophia were two girls who Sophia introduced in a whisper: "Lucy and Phoebe."

Both girls smiled. Phoebe was pretty, fair and small. Lucy, a taller, quiet-looking girl, had a shy manner.

A hush fell on the room, and Mrs. Neave, at the far end, spoke a grace. Mary Ann joined in the murmured "Amen", and there was a scraping of chairs as they all sat down and the servants moved into the room carrying dishes.

Mary Ann scarcely noticed the food, except to watch that she did not eat too fast for good manners; or too slowly; or reach for things across the table. Several dishes passed by her because she was too shy to ask for them. The teacher at the end called back a dish of carp and told Mary Ann, "Try this. It's good."

Sophia turned to the teacher: "Mrs. Corelli, Mary Ann is to have singing lessons with you. She is quite in *love* with music and wishes to become an opera singer."

Mary Ann blushed and looked at her plate. She

hadn't expected her confidence to Sophia to be passed on so publicly. And whatever would Mrs. Corelli think? Would she be dismissive, like Mary Ann's parents?

But Mrs. Corelli did not look surprised or disapproving. "I know Mary Ann is to have lessons," she said, "and I shall hear her sing this afternoon, after our deportment lesson."

But before Deportment came half an hour of French Conversation with Mrs. Neave.

"*Je ne comprends pas*," whispered Sophia as they followed a group of older girls into the front classroom. "Our most useful phrase."

"Here's another," said Lucy, pretending boredom: "*Le Français m'ennuie à mourir*."

They laughed. But Lucy, it turned out, was excellent at French: Mrs. Neave's best pupil. She could both speak and write the language well. Mary Ann's French was limited to what she had learned at her day school, and she struggled to keep up. She was relieved that Phoebe also seemed to be having trouble.

Phoebe preferred their next lesson. The anxiety left her face as they returned to the dining room, where the central space had been cleared of furniture to make room for Deportment and Dancing with Mrs. Corelli.

Mrs. Corelli was a large woman who moved with surprising lightness and grace. She was dressed dramatically in an emerald green gown that Mary Ann much admired.

Mary Ann had thought learning how to stand up and sit down in a hooped skirt, how to curtsy, how to walk, would be boring, but Mrs. Corelli made it fun.

"Imagine, girls," she said, "that you are out walking in the street, wearing a hooped skirt. If you bounce along, like this" – she began walking in a jaunty way, and they giggled – "your skirt will set up a rhythm of its own and you will not be able to control it, especially in a strong wind. And what if you sit down?"

She flumped onto a chair so that her skirt stuck up at the front, revealing striped stockings which Mary Ann suspected she had worn especially to make them laugh.

They promenaded around the room, careful to hold themselves erect, then practised sitting down and standing up, and taking a man's arm – Mrs. Corelli acting the part of the man.

"Lightly, child!" she exclaimed, when it was Mary Ann's turn. "Do not *clutch*."

Mary Ann was embarrassed. It did not seem to her at all a comfortable way to walk, and she hoped no man would ever offer her his arm. She was relieved when they finished the lesson with a dance: a minuet. There was a harpsichord in the corner of the room, and Mrs. Corelli played, glancing up to watch them. The older girls took the man's part, and Mary Ann found herself dancing with a tall girl named Emma whose limp hold made her own steps uncertain. She watched Phoebe, who looked as if she was born to dance.

"Oh, I love the minuet!" Phoebe exclaimed afterwards. "I can't wait to be old enough to go to balls!"

There was now a break from lessons, and the girls, who all looked pink and hot, fanned themselves as they queued for lemonade. Mrs. Corelli took two glasses and summoned Mary Ann.

"We shall take these up to the music room and I'll hear you sing."

"Oh! Now?"

Mary Ann was alarmed. What would Mrs. Corelli think of her singing? And *what* would she ask her to sing? Perhaps something difficult.

But when they reached the music room Mrs. Corelli looked through a collection of songs and asked, "Now, what do you know? 'Nymphs and Shepherds'? 'On Greenland's Coast'?"

"Oh, yes! Both. I mean – yes, I like 'Nymphs and Shepherds'."

"Good."

She put the music on the stand and sat down at the harpsichord and began to play. Mary Ann came in on time, but tentatively. It was a while before she gained confidence and sang louder.

"*In this grove,*

In this grove let's sport and play,

Let's sport and play…"

She was enjoying herself now, and as she continued she almost forgot she was being tested.

"Sacred to ease and happy love,

To music, to dancing and to poetry…"

When she reached the end she saw that Mrs. Corelli was pleased.

"You have a lovely natural voice," she said. "Soprano. I'm glad you are to have lessons. You will learn to control your breathing and to sing from *here* –" She put a hand on her midriff. "You will have lessons with me once a week and you will also join the choir. And I'm sure Mrs. Neave will want you to take part in our concert in September."

"A concert!"

"Every September we invite parents and visitors to the school. There is a display of work – needlework, drawing and such – and a concert with recitation, singing and playing."

"I should love to be in the concert," said Mary Ann. And she thought: perhaps, if I sing well, Mama will believe that I could become an opera singer.

She knew her father was less antagonistic to this idea than Mama. He was a bit of a singer himself, and it was his mother – her Grandmama Giffard – from whom Mary Ann had inherited her voice, and who had taken her to the opera for the first time and inspired in her the ambition to perform. She remembered how they had sat high up in the gallery and seen the singers far below on the candlelit stage – a jewelled tableau in a circle of light – and heard their voices soaring. Grandmama Giffard had died last year, but Mary Ann remembered her with love and gratitude.

"We will try 'Nymphs and Shepherds' again," said Mrs. Corelli. "But first, let us talk about breathing…"

Mary Ann left after half an hour and joined the others, who were reading around the group: an improving text on the subject of modesty.

Later, after supper, lagging a little behind the other three on their way to the dormitory, she had reached the first floor when she heard singing. Someone was singing 'Nymphs and Shepherds' in an easy, absent-minded way, humming over forgotten words – and she had the feeling that whoever it was had heard her practising with Mrs. Corelli and picked up the song by ear. The voice was a woman's, untrained, clear and pleasant, like those of some of the ballad singers Mary Ann loved to hear in the streets near her home.

Who could it be? The sound did not come from the music room but from a room next to the back stairs – a room Sophia hadn't bothered to mention.

She did not dare open the door; and when she hurried to join the other three on the second floor she was caught up in a flurry of gossip and giggles and forgot to ask them about it.

CHAPTER THREE

Jenny

Monday, 28th May, 1764

Dear Harriet,

I can scarcely believe it is already a month since I came here to Chelsea. I told you in my last letter how very much I liked the school and I am still of the same mind. Mrs. Corelli is so kind as to say that she thinks well of my singing and that I am developing a stronger voice already. Mr. Ashton, who teaches the harpsichord, is also pleased with my efforts. He takes us for Music and also Mathematics.

I am the best of friends with the three girls I share a room with. All four of us have harpsichord lessons, and Sophia and I are both in the choir. Sophia is full of gossip and plans: she is our leader. Phoebe is amiable and follows Sophia's view in everything. As for Lucy, Sophia teases her that she is so clever she will not get a husband. Lucy has a collection of shells and minerals which she keeps in a case under her bed (to the annoyance of the maids who try to sweep there). Although she is shy, she is witty and often makes us laugh.

I have written to Mama and expect she has told you that we read together in class every day, and write essays, and Mrs. Neave also teaches us Geography. There is a splendid globe, like the one Papa bought for George, but larger. We do needlework, which I like less, but Phoebe produces exquisite work; her stitches are so fine they can scarcely be seen.

We also go out to take the air, and on these occasions we are expected to behave in a ladylike manner; only sometimes we are so excited that it is difficult not to exclaim or dart about. Last Saturday, on our half-holiday, a party of us went to the Chelsea Bun House, which sells the most delicious sugared buns and cakes — you would love it, Harriet — but Lucy was in even more delight over the collection of curios and antiques which forms a small museum within the shop. We saw some extraordinary objects there, among them cuttlefish bones, and fossils, and a stuffed lizard.

On Sundays we go in file to church. The church is nearby, in Chelsea Walk, and is ancient; it has been here since Chelsea's beginnings. Inside, we listen to very long sermons. They are exceedingly dull. But we behave ourselves well and are seen to advantage by our neighbours, and that pleases Mrs. Neave. Of course we also sing hymns, which I enjoy.

There is another person here who likes to sing: one of the maids. Her name is Jenny. I heard her singing "Nymphs and Shepherds".

Mary Ann paused, and put down her pen. Perhaps it would be best not to write too much about Jenny. Harriet would undoubtedly share the letter with Mama, and their mother might not like the idea of Mary Ann making a particular friend of one of the maids.

She remembered her first evening, when she had heard the singing, and how she had seen Jenny the next morning, coming out of the room on the first floor, her arms full of clean, folded bed linen. The open doorway behind her had revealed a storage room containing shelves and baskets and a linen press. Jenny was humming to herself, and Mary Ann had known at once that here was her singer from the night before.

Without thinking, she exclaimed, "Oh! It was you!" The maid looked startled, and Mary Ann explained,

"I heard you singing yesterday: 'Nymphs and Shepherds'. I'd been practising it with Mrs. Corelli."

Jenny smiled. "I like to learn the young ladies' songs. They're different to the ballads I hear in the streets."

"Do you come from Chelsea?"

"Yes. My mother has a room on the waterfront, by the ferry. There's a tavern near our house, the Half Moon: I sing there some nights. And at the Duke of York."

Mary Ann was impressed. Jenny was a performer! She much admired the girl's looks: her dark eyes and tall, slender figure. She thought Jenny a finer-looking girl than any of the young ladies at the school. She said shyly, "I should like to hear you."

Jenny laughed. "Oh, I don't think so, Miss – not in a tavern." She shifted her bundle of linen and said, "I must see to my work, or Mrs. Price will be after me."

"The housekeeper?"

"Yes."

She knocked at one of the dormitory doors opposite and, receiving no answer, went in.

It was a while before they spoke to one another again, but Jenny always acknowledged the younger girl with a smile, and Mary Ann felt that they had become friends. A week or two later, when the choir had been talking about Ranelagh Gardens, Mary Ann asked Jenny if she had ever been there.

"Oh, yes, Miss! Not as a visitor. That costs two and sixpence; even more on firework nights. But my cousin Nick plays the fiddle, and sometimes he'll go in and play for the crowds in the gardens. Last time he took me with him and I sang. We made a hatful of money before the stewards moved us on. You'd love the Gardens, Miss; all the great folk go there. And the lights! It's like Paradise..."

Mary Ann brought her attention back to her letter.

I'll be home in less than a fortnight, for Whitsun, she wrote. *And George too. We shall all have so much to tell each other. I am glad to hear your news from home, and* especially that Papa expects success from his new venture. If he is in good spirits when I come home, do you think he'll take us to the Tower to see the animals? I do so love to go.

Till then, dear Harriet, I remain,

Your devoted sister,

Mary Ann Giffard

CHAPTER FOUR

Two Prodigies

The girls all went home for a week's holiday at Whitsun. Sophia, tossing chemises and stockings into her bag, made a great show of despair at the prospect of being parted from her friends.

"I don't know how I shall *endure* the holiday without you all! My brothers are *odious* and delight in provoking me. The week will seem far too long."

Mary Ann knew Sophia well enough by now not to

take all this too seriously. And Lucy said, "Well, I shall be glad to go home and see my cats and not have to think about lessons for a week."

"Oh, Lucy! You are heartless!" protested Sophia. "Mary Ann, will *your* brother be home? Is he as maddening as my two?"

Mary Ann said yes, he was, because that seemed to be the thing to say. In fact, she rather enjoyed George's company and had always been closer to him than to Harriet, who was seven years older than her.

"Lucy is lucky to be an only child." Phoebe, who also suffered from brothers, was rolling stockings into pairs.

A bell rang far below, signalling breakfast, and all four of them shrieked in alarm and flung a few more items into their bags before hurrying downstairs.

A buzz of chatter enlivened the queue as they filed into the dining room.

"Did you hear about those extraordinary children from – where was it? – somewhere in Austria?"

"Salzburg," said an older girl near Mary Ann. "The Mozarts."

"Such amazing musicians!"

Mary Ann listened eagerly to the gossip. She heard that there were two Mozart children, a boy of eight and a girl of twelve, and both were such gifted musicians that they had taken London by storm. They had arrived in the city with their parents only five weeks ago and had already been invited twice to the palace to play for the King and Queen.

"Of course the King loves music, and the Queen sings…"

"The King was enchanted with them, especially the little boy –"

"They say the boy composes and plays his own works. At such a young age! It is amazing."

"And the girl plays the harpsichord with brilliance…"

It seemed that there had been a concert at Spring Garden on Tuesday at which these "prodigies", as their father described them, had performed.

"Oh! I wish we could have gone!" exclaimed Mary Ann.

Lucy widened her eyes. "At half a guinea a ticket? I think not."

But after breakfast Mrs. Neave asked all the music students to stay behind. She told them about another concert – one they might be able to afford.

"I am arranging our annual visit to Ranelagh," she said. "There is to be a charity concert there in aid of a new hospital on Friday the 29th of June. The music is sure to be popular pieces that you will know, and this will be an opportunity – the first for some of you – to see Ranelagh Gardens. I shall enquire about tickets after the Whitsun holiday, when I know how many of you are coming. If you wish to be included in our party, please ask your parents for five shillings, and bring the money with you when you return to school. Don't forget."

As if we would, thought Mary Ann. And Sophia said, "Let's all go! It'll be such fun!"

"Don't let Mrs. Neave hear you say 'fun'," said Lucy, and Sophia put a hand over her mouth and pulled a face. "Fun" was a word used by young men about town, not by young ladies.

"What fun!" exclaimed George, when Mary Ann met him at home later that day and told him about the concert. "Ranelagh is all the rage, I hear."

"*Everyone* will be there," Mary Ann agreed, and sighed theatrically, Sophia-style. She meant everyone of consequence: the gentry, perhaps even royalty. "It will be quite divine!"

"Oh! *Quite* divine!" George, grinning, hopped out of reach as she went to hit him. They had all been teasing her, ever since she got home, about her new way of talking. She'd picked it up from Sophia without noticing, and now it had become second nature.

Her mother did not object.

"I'd rather Mary Ann spoke in that way than copied some of the girls at her old day school," she told a smirking George and Harriet. "And see how well she looks, and how she carries herself! I'm pleased with the change in her."

They were all impressed with the improvement in Mary Ann's harpsichord playing, and with Mrs. Corelli's comments on her singing. Mary Ann had chattered all the way home about the school, the teachers, her friends, and her music lessons.

"I do so love being there," she said. "And Mama, I need five shillings for the concert at Ranelagh! And my shoes are shabby – the ones I wore last summer…"

"George needs books and new clothes too," said her mother, "and Harriet must have a whole new wardrobe now she is engaged to Mr. Browne."

But none of this was a problem. When her father came home, Mary Ann dropped him a perfect curtsy, and he laughed with pleasure and took her hand and then scooped her into a hug. "My little girl! You are quite a lady already!"

He approved a visit to Cheapside for "shopping", as the ladies liked to call it.

"When the *Calliope* comes in – any day now – we'll be rich," he said. "You'll be in fine feather then, Harriet; more than a match for any son of Walter Browne." He winked above Mary Ann's head at her mother. "This'll show the old lady."

His wife gave a little shake of her head to silence him. But Mary Ann knew what he meant. "The old lady" was her other grandmother, her mother's mother, Mrs. Eleanor Causey, who was now a widow and lived in Kensington. Grandfather Causey had been a lawyer, and he and his wife had always disapproved of John Giffard because he gambled and took financial risks. They believed he could not give their daughter the security and respectability she deserved. Susan Causey had married him against their wishes, and had never been forgiven. So the Giffard children rarely saw their grandmother and Mrs. Causey was almost a stranger to them.

Their mother and Harriet began talking about silks and muslins, and which colours might suit Harriet's complexion. Mary Ann and George went down to the kitchen, chatted to the servants, wheedled some sweetmeats from Cook, and fussed old Bullet. They ended up in the small garden, where George climbed the apple tree and Mary Ann, despite her stiff skirts, followed him. They sat companionably, eating their pastries.

"Papa's in high spirits," said George. "Better make the most of it."

"What's this ship?"

Mary Ann did not really understand what her father did for a living. There was nothing to see, no merchandise to handle. His dealings involved investments and returns, and sometimes losses, and his mood would go up or down in tune with them.

"The *Calliope*?" said George. "She went out to West Africa last year. I don't know what the cargo was, but he was persuaded it was a good investment. She's on her way back from the Caribbean now."

"From the *Caribbean*?" Mary Ann had been making good use of the globe in her Geography lessons at school. "But you said the ship went to Africa."

"They buy slaves in Africa," George explained, "and sell them in the Caribbean. They're needed to work on the sugar plantations."

"How cruel – to seize people."

"They are not seized; not by Englishmen. Other Africans sell them to the traders. Papa told me."

Mary Ann thought of Lady Fanshawe, who lived at Number Five, Chelsea Walk. She had a black servant, a boy of about George's age. But that boy was not a slave, was he? He could not be, surely, not in England.

For a while she remained troubled about the *Calliope*, but before long it went out of her mind as she was caught up in a round of social events. They took tea with the Brownes. They went to the Tower of London's menagerie and saw lions, elephants, camels and a zebra. They went to Cheapside and chose materials to be made up into clothes for Harriet and

George and they ordered new summer shoes (pale soft leather with gilt buckles) for Mary Ann. One fine sunny day they made up a party with Mr. Browne and his sisters and walked in Kensington Gardens; and Mary Ann thought of her grandmother, who lived alone nearby, and wondered if she regretted the rift with her family.

The warm weather continued after Mary Ann returned to school. She became aware, almost for the first time, of the garden at the rear of the house. It was larger than the one at home, and laid out with paths and shrubs and sweet-smelling herbs that released their scent when her skirts brushed against them. Some steps there led down to the basement where the kitchen servants worked.

Her friend Jenny always entered the house that way, along with the other servants. But Jenny spent much of her time in the main part of the house, cleaning the rooms, bed-making, folding and sorting laundry.

One hot afternoon, a day or two after their return, when the girls were sketching in the garden, Mary Ann was sent indoors to fetch her straw hat. She ran upstairs. The first floor landing was deserted, but the door to the linen-storage room was ajar, and she saw a flicker of movement inside. That must be Jenny! She knocked, and pushed the door open at the same time.

"Oh!"

Jenny was behind the door, and both girls jumped, startled. But Jenny flushed scarlet – a guilty flush, as if caught out.

Mary Ann took in the scene. There was a basket on the floor – evidently Jenny's own basket, for her gloves and shawl were inside it. Jenny had been crouching, about to push something – a bundle of linen – under the shawl. She stood trapped, holding the linen. It was obvious that she'd intended to steal it.

Mary Ann, shocked and disillusioned, stared and felt herself going red in her turn.

Jenny unrolled the bundle, revealing it to be two pillowcases.

"Please, don't tell Mrs. Neave!" she begged.

CHAPTER FIVE

Maria Anna

"But – why?"

Mary Ann's disappointment in Jenny felt like a blow. She'd thought so highly of her. She did not want to believe her friend was a thief.

"It's my sister." Jenny folded the pillowcases and replaced them on a shelf. "She's ill – wasting away – spends most of her time in bed. And our bed linen at home is coarse stuff…"

At once Mary Ann felt both sorry and relieved. Jenny only wanted some comfort for her sister. She was not really a thief – or not such a bad one.

"You won't tell?" Jenny asked again.

"No…no, of course not," said Mary Ann, adding awkwardly, "I hope your sister will soon be well," although she thought "wasting away" didn't sound hopeful at all.

"Bless you!" Jenny's face cleared.

Mary Ann remembered her sun hat, and turned to go upstairs. Her faith in Jenny was restored – although since Jenny's basket was so close to the shelf with the pillowcases on it, she could not help wondering if they would find their way into it again.

But that was not her concern; and she had other things to think of. At the end of the week Mrs. Neave received the tickets and programme for the concert at Ranelagh Gardens. The programme gave details of the music to be played.

"A favourite chorus in *Acis and Galatea*," she told

the girls, "'O the Pleasure of the Plains'…the Song and Chorus in *Alexander's Feast*…and a surprise, which I think will please you: the two children of Mr. Mozart will perform on the harpsichord and organ –"

She must have known from the intake of breath that went around that this was what interested the girls most.

She read aloud to them from the programme: "The celebrated and astonishing Master Mozart will perform several fine select pieces of his own composition… which have already given the highest pleasure, delight and surprise to the greatest judges of music in England and Italy," she looked up, "…and they say that Master Mozart is the most amazing genius that has appeared in any age…"

"I cannot wait to see him!" Sophia exclaimed.

The four of them were in their dormitory, trying on their best gowns and considering whether anything new needed to be urgently requested from home.

"And *her*!" said Mary Ann. "I want to see *Miss* Mozart. They say she sings and plays the harpsichord, and she is just our age."

"I heard she is very pretty," said Phoebe. "And that Master Mozart is so small he has to sit on a cushion and even then he can scarcely reach the keys."

"How sweet!"

"And we'll hear *Acis and Galatea*," said Sophia. "I love that chorus."

She broke into song, and Mary Ann joined her:

"O the pleasure of the plains!
Happy nymphs and happy swains…"

Mrs. Corelli put her head around the half-open door. "You're in good voice, girls! Would you like to learn some more music from *Acis and Galatea* before we go to Ranelagh?"

"Oh, yes!" Mary Ann and Sophia agreed. And Phoebe, twirling in her sea-green gown, exclaimed, "Mrs. Corelli, we are *so* excited! Will we be able to walk in the gardens at dusk and see the lights?"

"We will," said Mrs. Corelli, "if we have fine weather."

The weather was kind to them. The girls and their teachers, dressed in silk gowns and furnished with fans for the heat in the Rotunda and light shawls to protect them from the evening air, made their way in a chattering crocodile along the riverside path to the landing stage. There they embarked in two boats and were taken to the river entrance of Ranelagh. It was a voyage of less than a mile and took no more than ten minutes, but for Mary Ann, as they approached the famous gardens, it was one she knew she would always remember. She gazed out at the river, glinting in the sunlight and crowded with small boats. They passed the waterfront gate of the Physic Garden and the grand steps and gates of the Royal Hospital, and in no time were in a queue of boats waiting to disembark at Ranelagh.

"Oh!" exclaimed Mary Ann. "The temple!"

Inside the gardens, not far from the gates, a Grecian temple of white stone stood amongst trees. This was the Temple of Pan; the older girls had told them about it. Gentlemen and ladies, festive in bright summer clothes, were strolling along the paths and in and out of the temple.

It took a while for the two boat-loads of girls and teachers – sixteen people in all – to come ashore. Mrs. Corelli drew the girls to one side while Mrs. Neave showed the tickets to the steward at the gates; and then they were inside, walking in pairs – Mary Ann was with Lucy – along a gravel path that led first to the Temple of Pan. This proved to be less mysterious at close quarters. It contained stone seats and was clearly a meeting point, with people coming and going and greeting each other with bows and cries of delight. The path led on beneath shady trees – elms and yews – towards the formal gardens nearer the house. The Rotunda could be glimpsed through the trees, looking like some monument of Ancient Rome. They passed a lawn cut in an odd shape – "an octagon", said Lucy – and a flower garden full of lilies and roses which Mrs. Neave insisted they stop to admire, although Mary Ann longed to move on.

In front of the Rotunda was an ornamental canal with what seemed to be a Chinese pagoda on it; but as they came closer this was revealed to be an elaborate roofed bridge painted in red, blue and gold and with space for people to gather on or wander about. All the younger girls wanted to cross the bridge, but some of the older ones affected boredom and walked around the path to meet them. The bridge and all the walks were full of people, and Sophia commented continually on the fashions and hairstyles.

"I do so admire that grey hair powder," she sighed. "I long to have my hair powdered, but Mama says I must wait till I am grown up. Oh! *Mes amies, regardez* that gown!"

But Mary Ann and Lucy were caught up in amazement at the sight of the Rotunda with its great circle of windows, high up, and an arcade running all around the building.

Mrs. Neave ushered them towards one of the grand entrances. They passed between two great pillars into a central space that took Mary Ann's breath away: a huge circular room hung with chandeliers that sparkled with candlelight, and at the centre a soaring column containing a fireplace – filled with flowers on this warm evening. Tilting her head back, she saw the circle of windows from the inside, high above a double ring of boxes. The orchestra, where the musicians were already warming up their instruments, was across the room. The floor was laid with matting, and this softened the sound of many footfalls as people promenaded, talking and greeting friends. There were smells of perfume, sweat, hair wax, flowers and coffee. The room was filling with more and more people, and Mary Ann felt, all around her, a gathering sense of eagerness and anticipation.

"We have two boxes on the upper tier," Mrs. Neave

said. And she shepherded her charges away from the concourse and up a staircase to a circular gallery with numbered doors.

Each box was big enough for seven girls and a teacher, with a table for their refreshments. Mary Ann was with Mrs. Corelli, who sat with three of the older girls while the younger ones squeezed past to sit in a row at the front: Sophia, Phoebe, Mary Ann and Lucy. From up here they had a view side-on to the orchestra and could see the musicians moving about, some talking, some seated and tuning their instruments. Behind the three tiers of orchestra seats the pipes of the organ rose to the ceiling. There was no sign yet of the Mozart children.

Below, the floor of the hall was full of people walking in sedate circles around the room. But now a few of them were beginning to move towards the ground floor boxes, and Mary Ann saw that the musicians and choir had taken their places and the conductor had appeared. The performers were dressed in bright clothes, the men in powdered wigs and jackets trimmed with lace and braid, the ladies in low-necked silk gowns, their hair powdered in white or grey and entwined with jewels that winked as the light caught them.

As the music began, the people below paused to look up. Some clapped or cheered, and one or two called out to certain performers and received a wave in reply. The music was the promised chorus from *Acis and Galatea* by Mr. Handel. Mary Ann listened and watched, noting every detail of how the female singers moved and held themselves.

All the music that followed was of a familiar, cheerful kind, and received with frequent loud applause from the audience. A worthy-looking gentleman appeared and spoke about the benefits to be gained from the proposed lying-in hospital and thanked people for their support; but the school party, eager for the Mozarts, paid little attention. Mrs. Neave looked in through the door of the box and asked what refreshments they would like for the interval, and went off to order tea, lemonade and bread and butter. The speaker retired, to applause.

Mary Ann, watching intently, was the first to see the Mozart family appear: the little boy, the girl, and a man who must be their father. She nudged Lucy and Phoebe on either side of her. "Look! They're here!"

More applause broke out as the Mozarts were introduced. Nannerl and Wolfgang, the children were called. The boy, Wolfgang, in a bright blue jacket, took his place at the organ: a tiny figure, dwarfed by the soaring pipes above him. He began to play a piece, they were told, of his own composition.

"Amazing!" murmured Mrs. Corelli, as the music filled the hall. "To compose such work at only eight years old!"

It was not until the second half of the concert that Miss Mozart performed. She moved to sit at the harpsichord: a slim, fair girl, straight-backed, wearing a green and white dress with a high neckline edged with coral-coloured lace, her hair drawn up in tight curls and decorated with coral flowers. Mary Ann admired her looks, and when the girl began to play she realized why Mr. Mozart had described her as a "prodigy". She knew, from her own practice, how difficult the piece was, and yet this girl made it seem effortless.

When she finished, to a roar of applause, her brother took her place at the harpsichord and Nannerl sang. Her voice was clear, high and sweet: a good voice – but not as good as mine, Mary Ann realized with surprise and some pleasure. It was obvious that the harpsichord was Nannerl's forte. She joined her brother at the instrument and the two of them played a fast, demanding piece together, their hands crossing and uncrossing, their own and each other's, so fast they could scarcely be seen.

At the finale they stood up and bowed to the enthusiastic crowd. Even from this distance Mary Ann could see the little boy's impish face and the girl's demure smile. She looked around and saw all the boxes full of cheering people.

She turned to Mrs. Corelli, behind her. "Oh, I *wish* I could play like that! And sing in public! I'd love to be Nannerl – but what a strange name!"

"Yes." Mrs. Corelli smiled. "That's what her family calls her. I heard that her proper name is Maria Anna."

"Maria Anna?" Mary Ann looked across at the girl, and Lucy said, "That's Mary Ann! Like you!"

I *shall* be like Maria Anna, thought Mary Ann. I'll work and practise every day. And she imagined herself there, with the orchestra, the lights shining on her and applause sounding from all around.

The concert ended with "God Save the King", and everyone stood up and sang.

And then it was over. There was shuffling, coughing and scraping of chairs. A slow movement of people began towards the exits. When at last she emerged into the night air, Mary Ann saw that it was dark, and all the lamps had been lit in the gardens. The Chinese bridge was lit up, the lamps reflected on the water in discs of shifting light; and coloured lanterns were hung from trees along the pathways. The girls gazed around, entranced.

"Girls! Stay together! Take care!" said Mrs. Neave.

The crowd emerging from the Rotunda divided, most people turning towards the King's private road, from where their carriages would take them home across Pimlico marshes to London. The school group joined those who were travelling by boat. This meant walking back along the tree-lined path that wound through the gardens, now lit all the way with lanterns. The brightness of the lamps made the darkness beyond them mysterious, as if the gardens had expanded to become a limitless domain. The Temple of Pan glowed white near the waterfront gates, and bright nymph-like figures in silken gowns could be seen moving inside.

The others chattered and giggled, but Mary Ann

was quiet, overcome by the wonder of the occasion. In her imagination she was onstage, Maria Anna and Mary Ann merged into one.

When they reached the house in Chelsea Walk and went inside, they were greeted by Mrs. Price with cups of chocolate and a warm fire in the dining room. Mary Ann sipped her chocolate, her mind still full of the sounds of singing, music and clapping, the glitter of the chandeliers and the sheen of silk. Mrs. Neave passed her a small printed card: one of the tickets for the concert. Each of the girls had one.

"A souvenir," said Mrs. Neave.

The ticket was illustrated with an engraving. It showed a woman – a goddess, or nymph – dressed only in her long hair and a wisp of drapery. In the background was a Pan figure playing reed pipes.

"I shall keep mine in my book of picture cards," said Lucy.

Mary Ann had no such book with her at school. Instead, when they went to their dormitory, she slid her ticket halfway into a crack in the wooden panelling beside her bed.

I'll be able to take it out and remember and be inspired, she thought.

But next day something happened that put all thoughts of Ranelagh and Maria Anna Mozart out of her mind.

CHAPTER SIX

News from Home

It was Saturday morning. The girls were at their first lesson of the day – Arithmetic – when a maid came in and spoke quietly to Mr. Ashton.

"Mary Ann," he said – and she stood up, her heart beat quickening. "You are to go to Mrs. Neave's office immediately."

She left, catching puzzled glances from her friends, and tapped on Mrs. Neave's door. Surely she'd done nothing wrong?

"Come in!"

Mary Ann opened the door, and was surprised to see her mother sitting opposite Mrs. Neave.

Mrs. Giffard did not look her usual self. Her hands, which she normally held still in her lap, were restless, pulling at the fingers of her gloves.

"Mama?" Mary Ann said uncertainly.

"Don't be alarmed, Mary Ann," said her mother. "No one is ill."

And Mrs. Neave told her, "You are to go home with your mother today. You may return on Monday morning."

"Oh – but…" Mary Ann thought of her singing lesson later that morning: Galatea's song about the dove. She'd been practising.

"You are excused lessons," said Mrs. Neave. "Go and fetch your cloak and shawl and anything else you wish to take with you."

Mary Ann went upstairs. When she came down

again with her outdoor clothes her mother was waiting in the hall.

"Mama, what is it?"

Her mother steered her outside, towards the landing stage on the riverside, before replying. "The ship – the one your father was expecting: it has sunk."

"Then…he has lost money?" said Mary Ann. She was accustomed to the ups and downs of her father's finances, but they were rarely down for long.

"Yes." Her mother spoke calmly, but there was a tremor in her voice that frightened Mary Ann. "We have lost nearly everything. I had no idea how much he had invested in this, and in another venture which has also failed. We have many creditors. We cannot live as we have been doing. We must economize."

It was a moment before Mary Ann realized the implications of this. Then she said in a voice of rising alarm, "Mama…?"

"You must leave Mrs. Neave's school," her mother said. She laid a hand on Mary Ann's arm. "Oh, not immediately, dear. You may stay till the end of July, of course; that is paid for. But we can't keep you there for another term."

"July! But there is to be the concert – the school concert – in September. You are to come. And I am to sing in it. And I love being there, Mama, you know that. I can't leave. I can't!"

"Oh, Mary Ann, I'm sorry," her mother said, "but there is simply no money. We'll talk about it at home. Your papa is there, and George is on his way. Look, there's a boat waiting. Compose yourself before we step aboard."

Out on the river and facing towards the City, Mary Ann turned round and watched the shoreline of Chelsea disappearing from view. She felt trapped, helpless. When she looked back at her mother her face was wet with tears.

The boatman pretended not to see. Her mother said, in a low voice, "We must do as your father thinks best, Mary Ann. You are not the only one to suffer. Think of Harriet – her position now as regards Mr. Browne."

But Mary Ann was too full of her own grief to care about Harriet and her fiancé. All she could think was that this boat was taking her farther and farther away from where she wanted to be: the house in Chelsea Walk.

CHAPTER SEVEN

"It's Not Fair!"

Mary Ann felt the tension in the house as soon as they arrived home. Even Betty, the kitchen maid, and the manservant Tom looked nervous – as well they might, Mary Ann thought, since they could lose their jobs.

Her father came out of his study to greet her and her mother. He had dark circles under his eyes, and through the half-open door Mary Ann could see papers spread about and a decanter of brandy.

"Well, Kitten!" he said, falsely hearty and using Mary Ann's baby name. "We must tighten our belts for a while. No doubt your mother has told you—"

"Papa!" Mary Ann could not help interrupting. "*Please* don't make me leave school!"

Instead of reprimanding her for her rudeness, her father looked almost apologetic.

"I've no choice, Kitten. Now, now –" he patted her shoulder – "tears won't help." He turned to his wife. "I shall go out to the coffee house; speak to friends. There may be contacts…"

He wants to escape us, Mary Ann thought.

She heard fast footsteps coming downstairs, and George burst into the room.

"Greetings, Little Sister!" He pulled a long face. "Oh – not you, too! Harriet is all of a mope upstairs, moving her things."

"Moving her things?"

Mrs. Giffard intervened: "I should have told you, Mary Ann. We have made space for you and Harriet in the blue room and will be letting your bedroom and the dressing room to a lodger."

"A lodger! Who?"

They had had financial problems before, but it had never come to this. And the blue room was tiny and overlooked the back yard and the privy.

"Do not shout, child. Remember your manners. We shall take a respectable woman. Perhaps even someone who might be able to play or sing a little, and could give you lessons…"

Mary Ann stiffened. She hated the proposed woman already.

"I must go and help Harriet," she said, and turned to the stairs. George followed her up.

Harriet had almost filled the press with her gowns. I don't know where mine will go, thought Mary Ann, but she didn't say so because her sister looked so miserable.

"This was not *my* idea," Harriet said defensively.

George crossed the room, leaned on the window sill and breathed in, wrinkling his nose. "Better keep this shut when the night-soil men come," he said.

"It's nothing to joke about, George," retorted Harriet. "*You* don't have to lose your room."

"Mine is smaller still! You would not get two beds in it."

This was true, but George's room was cosier, newly painted in yellow, and with a tiled fireplace. The blue room was shabby; even Amy, the lady's maid, had a fresher one: a small, neat space under the eaves.

"Make yourself useful, George," Harriet pleaded. "Fetch my box of shoes?"

When he had gone out, she turned to Mary Ann: "Father has written to Mr. Browne about my dowry." Her eyes brimmed. "It will be much diminished."

"Oh, Hatty!" For a moment Mary Ann put aside her own troubles. "If Mr. Browne loves you that will make no difference!"

"Have you been reading romances, Mary Ann? You know love has nothing to do with it. It is my fortune that matters."

"But – he must care for you."

Mary Ann thought dull Mr. Browne should consider himself lucky to have Harriet, who was pretty and well brought up and truly quite amiable most of the time.

"His family will not be in favour of the match now," said Harriet. "Whatever he may feel, they will talk him out of it."

George came in with Harriet's box and placed it on the floor. "You know, Hat, you might have my room most of the year. I'm only home for holidays."

"You *were*," said Mary Ann. "But now you'll be living at home, won't you?"

There was a silence. Mary Ann looked from George to Harriet, and the truth became plain to her.

"Oh! That's not *fair*!" she cried out.

She flew downstairs. "Mama! *Mama!*"

The parlour was empty. She ran on, down to the basement.

Her mother was in the kitchen, giving instructions

to Mrs. Wilson, the cook. She turned a shocked face to her daughter.

"Mama, if George is to stay at school why can't I?"

"Mary Ann, control yourself!"

Her mother took her by the shoulders, her fingers pinching, and steered her out of the kitchen and upstairs to the parlour.

"*Never* let me hear you shouting like that again! And in front of the servants! Has Mrs. Neave taught you nothing?"

"She will not have the chance now!" retorted Mary Ann.

Her mother slapped her face. Mary Ann's eyes watered from the sting and the humiliation. She began to cry in earnest. "It's not fair," she sobbed.

"Of course it is not," her mother said. "When was life ever fair to women? But your father is right. George's education must prepare him for a career in the City. He will have needs and responsibilities that you will never have. Don't imagine that life is easier for a boy. It is harder, more competitive. Your father would only take George away from that school as a very last resort, if we were penniless. Whereas…"

Whereas my education is unimportant, thought Mary Ann. Even so, she'd fight for it. She said, "I will make a better marriage if I can sing and dance and speak French and behave like a lady."

"A better marriage requires a larger dowry," her mother replied. "I'm sorry, Mary Ann, but there is nothing to be done. We must reduce our expenditure. We intend to sell some of my jewellery—"

"I could sell mine!" Mary Ann interrupted, eager to help.

Her mother brushed the offer aside, as if it was of no consequence. She sighed, and looked around the room, at the new flock wallpaper, the painted floor cover and the long green curtains with their gold tassels: all bought last year.

Mary Ann said tentatively, "We could ask Grandmama Causey."

At once her mother's face closed up. "You know I never approach your grandmother for help."

"But you might...just this once. She might *like* to help."

"I don't doubt she would *like* it," said Mrs. Giffard. "It would give her great satisfaction."

And then she was silent, as if she felt she had said too much. But Mary Ann understood. She knew that for her mother to ask for help now would mean to admit that she had been wrong to marry John Giffard, that he was as unreliable as her parents had said, that they had been right all along.

And she wondered if her mother *did* regret her marriage. Sometimes, in bed at night, she'd heard raised voices, doors slamming; and her father was often away on business.

Marriage was not something that Mary Ann looked forward to. To become an opera singer – that was her dream. And at Mrs. Neave's she'd felt she was on her way to achieving it.

"If I could have only the singing and harpsichord lessons?" she pleaded. "I don't mind about Geography and Arithmetic, or even Deportment…"

Her mother shook her head.

"Just one more term…the concert—"

"Oh, Mary Ann! Go and talk to Harriet. Don't pester me, *please*!"

They sat on Harriet's bed: Mary Ann, Harriet and George. Mary Ann was going through the contents of her jewellery box. There was a locket – a birthday present from her parents – a child-size silver bracelet, an amber brooch, a necklace of dark red stones.

"Garnets," said Mary Ann.

"Glass," said Harriet. "And you can't sell any of these. Mama would not hear of it."

"If they *were* garnets," said Mary Ann obstinately, "I might get eight guineas for them."

She remembered from Mrs. Neave's advertisement that the school cost twenty-one guineas a year. Seven guineas would buy her another term there, but she'd need extra for the music lessons.

Harriet took the box from her and closed the lid. "They are glass. And there is nothing any of us can do."

"But it's so unfair! Why should George stay at school and not me?"

"It's a great pity, but you have to see that Father's decision is entirely reasonable," said Harriet.

"And to be expected," agreed George – complacently, Mary Ann thought.

She punched him. "You told me you cared!"

"I *do* care! I'm sorry, truly I am! But I am the son and heir. That's the difference."

On Sunday there was more bad news. A letter came, delivered by a servant, addressed to Harriet. It was from Mr. Philip Browne, who told her that, with great regret, he felt it necessary to break off their engagement. Harriet, weeping, rushed upstairs to the blue bedroom and shut herself in. Her mother followed her. Mary Ann and George, listening nearby, could hear storms of tears from Harriet and soothing noises from their mother. Mr. Giffard kept out of the way in his study.

"She shouldn't waste tears on *him*," said George.

"No," agreed Mary Ann. "He's a toad." "Toad" was Sophia's favourite word for anyone she disliked, and Mary Ann wrinkled her nose, like Sophia, as she said it.

Mr. Browne had made Harriet unhappy, and that was reason enough to dislike him; but what Mary Ann would never have admitted, even to herself, was that she particularly hated Mr. Browne for having focused everyone's attention so exclusively on her older sister. Harriet emerged from her room red-eyed, pale and stricken, unable to eat or to speak above a whisper: the very picture of a jilted bride. Everyone was sorry for her. Later, when Mary Ann once again pleaded to be allowed to stay on at school (for she was to go back there in the morning and this was her last chance) all her mother would say was, "How can you be so selfish? Think of poor Hatty." The whole household, including the servants, was taken up with sympathy for Harriet's cause. No one had time for Mary Ann.

CHAPTER EIGHT

Tea with Mrs. Corelli

Back at school, in the dormitory, it was different. Mary Ann's friends had missed her, and worried about her, and no one knew why she had gone home so suddenly. When she told them her news, they surrounded her with all the sympathy and attention she had longed for at home.

"But that's *terrible*!" exclaimed Sophia.

And even quiet Lucy said, "You *can't* leave us. There

must be something we can do."

They all gathered round and tried to comfort her, and that made Mary Ann cry again.

"Mrs. Neave will help, surely?" said Phoebe.

"No." Mary Ann gulped back tears. She was certain that Mrs. Neave would not help, for how could anyone run a business at a loss?

"I shall talk to Mrs. Corelli," Sophia decided. "*She* won't want to lose you. You're our best singer by far."

"And a good advertisement for the school," Lucy pointed out.

But they all knew Mrs. Corelli was only an employee and could have no say in the matter.

"We're such a friendly little group here," Sophia said – making Mary Ann wail, "I *know*!" and cry even more – "I shall tell Mrs. Corelli that if you leave we might get some *toad* of a girl who can't even *sing*…"

No one had a solution, but their sympathy was comforting, and they even had some left over for

Harriet, though they were not shocked to hear that George would remain at his school.

"That is quite natural, Mary Ann," said Sophia. "Your education cannot be considered as important as your brother's."

"You can't call that unfair," agreed Phoebe.

"You *can*," said Lucy, "but it will not help. It's the way of the world, my mother says."

Everyone at school was kind. Mrs. Neave was especially concerned; and Jenny paused in her work to talk and sympathize.

Mrs. Corelli was determined to look on the bright side.

"You must put all this out of your mind for now, and concentrate on your work," she said. "We have the September concert to prepare for—"

"But I won't be *here* in September!"

Mrs. Corelli shook her head. "Now, Mary Ann, who knows what will happen? Your father's fortunes may have improved by then. We must be ready. And you are my best soprano among the younger girls. Now, what did you intend to sing? An air of Galatea's, wasn't it? And anything else?"

"Yes. Galatea. 'As when the dove…' I like that one. And 'Nymphs and Shepherds'?"

"The choir will sing 'Nymphs and Shepherds'. You'll be part of that." (Mary Ann wished it were true.) "What about 'When Daisies Pied and Violets Blue' for a solo? That's pretty, and would suit your voice. But first, let me hear the Galatea…"

Mary Ann tried hard to think only of the music, to forget her troubles. She sang:

"As when the dove
Laments her love
All on the naked spray;
When he returns
No more she mourns
But love the live-long day…"

Her voice broke on "mourns", and spoiled what

should have been the joyful crescendo of the next line. By the end of the song tears were streaming down her cheeks. "I won't be here to sing it!" she wept.

"But you must *learn* it!" insisted Mrs. Corelli. "How else can you be ready when occasion demands? If you are to be a performer, you must always be ready."

"My parents won't allow me to be a singer," said Mary Ann, determined to be sorry for herself.

"Then they are probably wise," Mrs. Corelli said. "It is a difficult choice, the stage, and very few succeed. Oh, Mary Ann! Your voice is quite gone with all this crying. Dry your tears, and come up to my room. I'll make tea."

Mary Ann had always been curious to see inside the teachers' private rooms, and she immediately felt more cheerful as she followed Mrs. Corelli upstairs to the second floor.

Mrs. Corelli's room was across the stairwell from the younger girls' dormitory, and opposite Mrs. Neave's suite. It was a fair size, but filled to overflowing with

Mrs. Corelli's possessions. There was a bed, a press, a cupboard, a music stand, a table and two chairs, cooking pots and a kettle. And all around the walls and on the mantelpiece and shelves were displayed playbills, engravings, open fans, a plume of feathers, a crimson shawl. The bed was curtained off, but the cooking area by the fireplace was open to the room.

Mrs. Corelli put the kettle on a trivet over the fire, then took a small key from a bag at her waist and unlocked a little black lacquered tea caddy. Mary Ann felt privileged to be given tea, which was so expensive.

"It's cosy here. I like it," she said, watching Mrs. Corelli measure a spoonful of tea into the warmed pot.

"But hardly what *you* are accustomed to?"

"Well…until Hatty and I were put together, I had a bedroom all to myself…"

"In a big house, with servants to wait on you?"

"Yes."

"I might have had the same, if I had not followed my heart."

Mary Ann had already noticed, in a frame on the wall opposite, a small painting of a young man, dark and slightly foreign-looking.

"Is that Mr. Corelli?" she asked.

"Yes." Mrs. Corelli placed two cups of tea on the table. The cups were cracked but pretty. Mary Ann's had medallions painted on it enclosing scenes of cupids and goddesses.

"My husband was a singer," Mrs. Corelli explained. "Italian. He had a fine voice and was much sought after by the opera companies."

"He was famous?" Mary Ann was entranced. "How did you meet? Where?" In her excitement she quite forgot to be deferential to her teacher.

Mrs. Corelli did not seem to mind the informality. "At Drury Lane Theatre," she said. "I was a singer too."

"Oh! I knew it!" exclaimed Mary Ann. Mrs. Corelli was no longer young, but she moved like an actress and her dress was always a little more flamboyant than you'd expect in a teacher. ("She knows how to wear a shawl," Sophia had said once.) "Were *you* famous?"

"A little, for a while."

She opened a drawer and brought out a green cloth-covered box. Inside were old tickets, advertisements, playbills, prints of engravings.

"Here is all my life, and my husband's, on the stage."

Mary Ann leafed through them: "...*The Beggars' Opera*...the part of MacHeath played by Enrico Corelli" ... "Enrico and Jane Corelli" ... "the celebrated Mr. Corelli..." ... "Mrs. Corelli excels as Margarita..."

"Oh! This is wonderful!" She sighed. "I wish I might do the same!"

"It did not last long," said Mrs. Corelli. "We had some good years. But now, you see, I am a widow, and my voice and looks are not what they were, and my home is this little room..."

"I *love* your room!"

Mrs. Corelli laughed. "So do I, my dear! It's my

haven. But you know, the stage is a difficult life without much reward for most people. And to achieve even a small success you must work hard, and practise daily, and above all be ready! Never give up hope."

A bell rang far below, and she stood up. "We shall practise again on Wednesday, and you will be in good voice and dry-eyed. Is that agreed?"

"Yes, Mrs. Corelli."

She went out. The bell meant it was time for the afternoon break, and the girls would be gathering in the dining room for lemonade. Well, she didn't need any; she'd had tea! She went into the dormitory and sat on her bed and pulled out the Ranelagh ticket from its crack in the panelling. She gazed at the nymph in her swirling drapery and Pan playing his pipes, and imagined just such a ticket announcing her own appearance as the nymph Galatea.

Mrs. Corelli had cheered her up and made her feel that anything was possible. She saw now that she needed to work to make her own fortune. If her parents could not pay, she must find the money for next term herself in the only way she knew: she must sing for the money.

CHAPTER NINE

Plans

"I guessed, the first time I saw her!" declared Sophia, when Mary Ann told the other three about Mrs. Corelli having been on the stage. "I said so to you, did I not, Lucy? I said, 'You can see from the way she moves that she is an actress'."

"But you haven't been inside her room," said Phoebe enviously. "You haven't seen the portrait of Mr. Corelli."

"No… We must find a way to be invited, all of us."

"Lose our voices?" joked Lucy.

They laughed. But they were jealous. Mary Ann knew it was not a good time to share with them her idea of singing to raise money for her fees. She had thought, at first, about a concert organized by the four of them, but she soon foresaw the difficulty of finding either an audience who would pay or a place to stage it. Even if it were allowed, it would be humiliating to perform at school and let everyone know that her parents could not afford the fees. She realized that she needed to do this by herself. She remembered the ballad singers she always liked to hear in the streets of London. Those women would have a hat on the ground, or an assistant who went in amongst the crowd asking for money. They must do well on market days.

But ballad singing was unthinkable. She was a merchant's daughter. She could not stand in the street and sing.

It was the next day, when she glanced out of the window during a Geography lesson, and saw Jenny hanging out washing in the garden, that the answer came to her. Surely Jenny would help! She sang in a tavern; she'd even sung at Ranelagh, with her cousin.

She waited until the next time she saw Jenny going into the laundry room alone, then followed her in and closed the door.

"Oh, Miss!" Jenny turned round. "You startled me!"

She'd had a slightly guilty manner ever since the affair of the pillowcases.

Mary Ann spoke quietly. "Jenny, I need your help. Will you be singing – performing – again soon?"

"Oh, yes, Miss!" Jenny's face cleared. "I'm going with my cousin to Ranelagh on Saturday week."

"To Ranelagh!" This was even better than Mary Ann could have hoped. Surely at Ranelagh, among so many wealthy people, she would earn enough money to keep her here at least one more term?

"It's a masquerade night," Jenny explained.

"Everyone will be masked, even the stallholders."

"Masks!" Mary Ann was enthralled. "Will *you* wear a mask?"

"Oh, yes – to blend in! It should be a good night: dancing and all sorts of entertainments going on till the small hours of the morning."

"Take me with you!" Mary Ann begged. "Let me sing too!"

"*You*, Miss?" Jenny looked horrified. "Oh – I couldn't – no, not you. It's not suitable… I'd be in trouble. And Nick, my cousin – he'd never agree."

"Please, Jenny, *please*! You know why. I need eight guineas for next term. There's no other way for me to earn it."

"You'd never get eight guineas, Miss."

"But I'd get something! It would be a start. And it would be secret. The masks. We'd be disguised." It seemed a chance she could not forgo.

"No." Jenny's face was set. "No, I daren't do it. I'm sorry."

"I helped *you*," Mary Ann said. "I never told anyone what I saw. Those pillowcases…"

She hated herself even as she spoke. It was wrong: blackmail. But it worked. Jenny looked wary.

"I'll ask Nick," she said. "I'll see him on Sunday. "But it'll be up to him, Miss, and I reckon he'll say no. Indeed, I'm sure he will."

Mary Ann waited. She was in a fever of impatience for the rest of the week, and could not attend to her lessons or to the gossip of her friends. But when she went for her next singing lesson with Mrs. Corelli she managed to put her anxiety aside and worked hard at the songs. These were important. Mrs. Corelli had told her that she must be ready at all times, and she was determined she would be: ready for Ranelagh. Mrs. Corelli was surprised and pleased, and praised her.

On Sunday Mary Ann was restless, biting her nails in church, wondering when Jenny would be back and when the two of them would have a chance to talk.

At last, when they were going in to supper, she caught a glimpse of Jenny in the back part of the house. Jenny saw her, and flicked a glance upwards, and Mary Ann broke from her friends, saying, "I forgot my handkerchief!" and darted upstairs.

Jenny, meanwhile, had hurried up the back stairs. They met on the first floor landing, near the linen room.

Jenny was breathless. "He says – yes!"

"Oh!" Mary Ann was so pleased that she flung her arms around the maid and hugged her.

Jenny seemed rather less delighted. "Fool that I am, I told him what a sweet voice you had, and he says the folks there will love it, a young one like you singing. But we need to get you out, and back again, without Mrs. Neave knowing. And that won't be easy."

Mary Ann hadn't even thought about the mechanics of her plan; gaining Jenny's agreement to it had been what obsessed her. Now she realized that she would be breaking the school rules by going out unauthorized and at night. She could be in serious trouble if Mrs. Neave found out – expelled, even. But then she had nothing to lose. Unlike Jenny.

"You must not tell your friends," said Jenny. "If you give even a hint to those tattle-boxes, we're finished. Do you understand? Promise?"

"I promise. Thank you, Jenny."

It would be a long week, she thought, keeping such a secret to herself.

CHAPTER TEN

Out at Night

It was Saturday morning – the day of the masquerade at Ranelagh Gardens.

"We'll go to Ranelagh after dark," said Jenny. She was folding sheets in the linen room, with an eye open for Mrs. Price, whose voice could be heard downstairs. "About half past ten."

"So late!" Mary Ann was always in bed by nine.

"Oh, people will arrive late," said Jenny, "and stay

till morning. These grand folk keep strange hours!"
She lowered her voice still further. "Can you slip out
without the other girls seeing?"

"I think so."

"Don't let them in on this. I'm risking my place.
You know that."

"Yes."

"Come down the back stairs and I'll be waiting.
I'll make some excuse to stay late in the kitchen. The
doors will be locked, but there's a window we can get
out of."

A window! Mary Ann felt nervous. She'd never
done anything like this before, but Jenny spoke as
if climbing out of a window was an everyday occurrence.
She nodded.

"I'll bring a mask for you. Wear something pretty."

"My best dress!"

"No, not that! But a bright colour. You've got a rosy
pink one, haven't you? And have some lace and
ribbons about you. But don't wear a hoop under your

skirt. And you'll need sturdy shoes – not those." She glanced down at Mary Ann's light-soled fabric slippers.

Mrs. Price appeared at the top of the stairs. "Jenny, are you –" She stopped in surprise at sight of Mary Ann. "The young ladies are all at their lessons, Miss."

"I – lost a book..." Mary Ann said, and darted away downstairs, terrified that their plan would be discovered. She slipped into Mrs. Neave's English lesson with a curtsy and downcast eyes, murmuring a similar apology, and receiving a reprimand.

"What are you up to?" Sophia demanded afterwards. "I saw you with Jenny. You keep chatting to her."

"No, I don't!" Mary Ann's heart hammered. "Well, not often. But she's my friend; you know that. She's kind."

To distract the others, she suggested a visit to the Bun House that afternoon. There were always teachers or older pupils willing to supervise a Saturday outing there. On the way they stopped at a haberdasher's, and Mary Ann bought some pink ribbon for her hair.

Later, after supper, she made an excuse of tidying the gowns hanging in the cupboard, and put her rose-sprigged cotton gown within easy reach, with a fringed shawl draped over it. She placed her shoes, with stockings rolled inside them, where she could find them in the dark. The cupboard door squeaked when you opened it, so she left it ajar and hoped no one else would close it.

The girls sat about in their chemises and combed their hair and talked about their day. They reminisced happily about the sugary buns they'd bought and the array of ribbons and lace at the haberdasher's. Mary Ann was quiet, but hoped the others would put it down to her unhappiness at the thought of leaving them all. If only she could tell them! But she'd promised Jenny, and probably it was safer this way.

"Let me comb your hair, Mary Ann!" Sophia begged; and Mary Ann agreed, and let Sophia twist it into curls and tie the new pink ribbons in it. She planned to leave them in at bedtime, as if by accident.

The clock on the first floor landing had just struck nine when Mrs. Neave put her head around the door and said, "Into bed now, girls."

"Oh, Mrs. Neave, it's still light outside!" protested Sophia.

"Then draw the curtains, child. You don't want to be tired for church tomorrow."

She went out, closing the door, and Sophia giggled and said, "I might as well be. I always sleep through the sermon."

"*So* dull!" agreed Phoebe.

But they allowed Mary Ann, who was nearest the window, to draw the curtains, and all wished each other goodnight and got into bed.

Mary Ann lay waiting. Sophia fell asleep quickly, as she usually did; her breathing soon became slow and steady. Then came the little snuffling sounds that Phoebe always made in her sleep. Lucy was quiet. But she was on the other side of the room, near the door, and Mary Ann knew she was a light sleeper.

She dared not move too soon.

She heard the clock strike ten. Was Jenny downstairs, in the kitchen? Probably all the servants were still there. She lay wide awake, waiting a while longer, to give the maids and teachers time to go upstairs to their rooms. She heard creakings, low voices; but at last the house seemed to be still, full of a soft breathing quiet.

She slid out of bed, went to the cupboard, and glanced at Lucy: dark hair on the pillow, face turned away. She took her gown off its hook, picked up her shoes, then opened the door. It made a faint click. When she looked back, Lucy had turned over, but she seemed to be asleep. Mary Ann crept out, closing the door softly behind her, and padded barefoot across the landing to the back stairs.

The stairs were pitch dark. She felt her way down a few steps, then stopped and put on her stockings and shoes. She slipped the dress on over her chemise and draped the shawl around her shoulders. The dress had a boned bodice and did not require stays, but she'd need Jenny's help to do it up.

The stairs creaked alarmingly as she moved down: one, two, three flights. And at the bottom there was a cold stone floor underfoot, and a chilly draught. She'd never been in the basement before. This was where the kitchen staff spent nearly all their time.

There was a door to her right, half open. She touched it, and heard Jenny's voice: "Who's there?"

"It's me: Mary Ann."

"Ah." Jenny sounded relieved.

Next moment a candle came alight, and Mary Ann saw the gleam of eyes. Jenny looked beautiful in a red dress, low cut, her dark hair in curls under a little tilted hat with a grey feather.

"Are you ready?" she asked.

"Yes. But can you help me do up my dress?"

She felt Jenny's hands at her back. "There." Jenny tied the shawl securely in place over it. "You'll need your hands free. What a fine pair we are!" She glanced at the window. "My cousin will be waiting – if you're sure you want to come?"

"Yes. Yes, of course!"

"Right." Jenny led her to the scullery window. There was a shallow stone sink under it, and a wooden table at the side. They hitched up their skirts and climbed onto the table. Then Jenny blew out the candle and Mary Ann felt her move away, into the sink, and heard the sound of the sash window being cautiously raised. Cool air flowed in.

"Follow me. And try not to make a sound climbing out. Mrs. Price's window is just above."

Mary Ann could see enough to know that Jenny was out through the window and down on the paving outside. She'd moved quickly, despite her full skirts, and Mary Ann realized it wasn't the first time she'd gone out this way. She struggled to follow: found her footing on the edge of the sink, turned, and went out backwards, Jenny's hands on her waist guiding her down.

Jenny pulled the window back into place, took Mary Ann's hand, and ran with her up the basement steps, then down the length of the dark garden, keeping close to the wall. She unlatched the tradesmen's gate at the end, and they both slipped out into Robinson's Lane.

A man was waiting in the shadows.

"Nick!" Jenny drew Mary Ann round to face him. "Here's our young lady: Mary Ann."

Nick was slim and tall, like Jenny. He wore a yellow spotted neckerchief and a black hat and carried a violin case on a strap across his body. He made a hint of a bow to Mary Ann, then said, "Let's find a boat."

They went to the waterfront, where the landing stage was thronging with people – to Mary Ann's surprise, for the hour seemed late to her.

Soon they were in a boat, being rowed across the dark water. Mary Ann shivered, despite her shawl. It was not such a fine evening as on her last visit, and there were spots of rain on the wind. But she grew warmer with anticipation as they came within sight of

Ranelagh and saw the gardens lit with thousands of lanterns, the white Temple of Pan gleaming from a distance, and lights all along the waterfront reflected and moving on the river, like stars. She heard music and, as they arrived at the landing stage, a busy hum of voices. People, some already masked, swept past, wafting perfume.

She had assumed that Nick and Jenny had tickets or performers' passes, and that they would all go in through the same gate as everyone else, but the two of them led her away from the gate, along the towpath and around the perimeter of the gardens, which were bordered by a fence and a high hedge.

There were fewer lights here, and it was muddy. She caught Jenny's hand. "Where are we going?"

"Ssh! Nick knows the way."

They stopped, and Mary Ann saw a break in the fence: a paling missing. Jenny at once squeezed through and, with a bit of rustling and a soft curse, disappeared from sight.

It was then that Mary Ann realized, all in a rush, that Nick and Jenny were not licensed to perform at the gardens, as she'd supposed; that they were breaking in; that they'd done this before; and that they could all end up in much worse trouble than she'd risked already by leaving school without permission.

"I don't think –" she began. But Nick said, "You next, Miss," and pushed her ahead of him through the gap. She felt the prickly branches of the hedge on her face and arms, and heard Jenny whisper, "There's a way through here. Bit of a squeeze. Mind yourself on the thorns."

Nick was behind her, and Jenny caught her from in front, and together they helped her through. No wonder Jenny had told her not to wear her best dress, Mary Ann thought.

They emerged onto a dark path amongst trees, faintly lit by lights farther along.

Nick stood up, adjusted his hat, and said, "Welcome to Ranelagh, ladies. Shall we find ourselves a pitch?"

CHAPTER ELEVEN

Masquerade

He took their arms, one on each side of him, and Mary Ann thought: a man has offered me his arm! How jealous Sophia would be! And she felt suddenly grown-up and grateful to Mrs. Corelli for the deportment lessons.

Now that they were inside the gardens, unchallenged, she began to feel less anxious. Nick and Jenny seemed quite carefree, chatting as they walked along the path.

Nick struck out confidently towards the lights and movement, and occasionally they passed groups of young men, or couples who whispered and laughed together. Most of them were masked. Some way off Mary Ann could see the Temple of Pan, where a constant movement of people flowed to and fro. Closer to hand, there were other attractions: a juggler, people in fancy dress: a man dressed as Punch, a woman in harem trousers and a flimsy chemise that shocked Mary Ann. All around were little booths with lanterns hanging outside, the candle flames flickering in the breeze. These sold sweetmeats and drinks.

Nick stopped by a natural arbour at the side of the path, where a lantern swung in the branches, and let go of the girls' arms. "This will do," he said. He opened the violin case and took out the instrument, and placed his hat on the ground.

Jenny produced masks: a black and gilt one for Nick, sparkling green for herself, and blue and silver for Mary Ann. Once her mask was tied in place

Mary Ann felt safer. No one would know her now.

Nick began to play: a sweet, romantic tune. And he looked the part, with his dramatic pose, the fiddle on his shoulder, the yellow neckerchief catching the light.

Jenny took Mary Ann to a stall and bought her a bag of sugared almonds. She also asked for three glasses of wine, and gave one to Mary Ann. "That'll wet your whistle," she said.

Mary Ann didn't like the taste of the wine, but she sipped it, for politeness' sake, as they walked back.

A few people had paused to listen to Nick's playing. Mary Ann heard a chinking of coins in the hat. Nick called to Jenny, "A song, sweetheart!" He began to play an air from *The Beggars' Opera* that Mary Ann knew; and Jenny stood beside him and sang, holding out her arms in dramatic gestures like the ladies at the opera and drawing cries of admiration from the gathering crowd. The gentlemen, who all seemed to go about in noisy groups, cheered and threw coins as the song ended. Jenny smiled and curtsied, the red dress sweeping the ground, her dark eyes shining.

"Encore!" someone – drunk, by the sound of him – shouted. But Jenny turned to Mary Ann and drew her forward. "Sing that dove song," she whispered. "Tell Nick; he'll know it…"

Nick did know it, and began to play Galatea's air, and Mary Ann sang – too softly at first to be heard over the wind and rustling leaves and drunken chatter of passers-by. But then a hush fell, and people listened, and her voice soared clear:

"As when the dove
Laments her love,
All on the naked spray;
When he returns,
No more she mourns,
But love the live-long day…"

At the end, as she curtsied, loud clapping broke out, and Mary Ann heard women's voices: "Such a sweet child!" "Another Miss Mozart, I do believe!"

They called for more – and Nick caught her eye and began to play the tune again.

The hat was filling nicely. When the crowd moved on, Jenny scooped up most of the contents and stowed it away in a pocket hidden beneath a slit in her skirt. Nick laid down the fiddle and put an arm around each of them.

"You were right, Jenny!" he said. "She sings like an angel. And I was right to tell you to bring her. The ladies love it!" He turned to Mary Ann. "What else do you know, sweetheart? Could you sing a duet with Jenny?"

They sang a few more songs – Mary Ann joining Jenny in familiar ballads, then one or other of them singing alone. Nick encouraged Mary Ann to sing her "operatic stuff" as he called it. "They like that." But when she tried to copy Jenny's extravagant gestures he shook his head at her. "Keep it sweet and simple," he said afterwards. "Suits you better."

And the people enjoyed it. The hat grew full, and once more Jenny transferred its contents to her pocket;

and Mary Ann sipped her wine between songs and thought the drink wasn't so bad after all – it made her feel a bit warmer as the night grew cool. Although it was spotting with rain, more and more people were strolling along the paths: groups of loud-voiced young men, or couples arm-in-arm.

When she was not singing, Mary Ann listened to snatches of conversation. She heard women talk of a lighted gondola on the canal, and of a row of little shops selling fans and other finery; and she could hear, from a distance, sounds of an orchestra playing dance music. She turned wistfully in its direction. She was glad her singing was appreciated, and that Nick was pleased with her, and especially glad to see the money dropping into the hat, but it seemed that much more was happening in the main part of the gardens, nearer the Rotunda, and she wished that they could go there. She wanted to see the Chinese bridge all lit up, and the gondola, and the dancers in their elaborate masks. But Jenny said no, they must stay here, and

Mary Ann guessed it was because they had broken in and must keep away from any stewards. It was so different from her last visit, and she felt disappointed.

Despite the cool weather the crowds did not lessen, and the revellers were becoming noisier and more drunken. Gangs of men lurched by, and Mary Ann felt afraid when they stared at Jenny in her red dress and shouted coarse remarks. She was sure that only the presence of Nick kept them safe. A fight broke out just ahead of them on the path, and a man, supported by his friends, was left with blood running down his face onto his shirt. Farther off, where the lamps petered out and little winding paths led in amongst dark trees, they heard occasional shrieks and scuffles, and once a young woman burst out and rushed past them, sobbing.

"We should go now," said Jenny, and Nick agreed. He bent to pick up the violin case – and at that moment two men sprang out of the darkness. Mary Ann saw one of them leap on Nick, and then the other pushed her to the ground. She landed hard, the breath knocked from her body, and hit her hand on something sharp. When she looked up, she saw Jenny grappling with the man, screeching, "Thief!" But he flung her down and scooped up the contents of the hat and was gone, in amongst the trees.

Jenny and Mary Ann both stood up. Nick's attacker had punched him to the ground and fled. He struggled up, cursing.

"Oh, Mary Ann – Miss! Are you hurt?" Jenny looked panic-stricken at the sight of her.

"No…only my hand – I may have cut it…" Mary Ann was trembling, on the brink of tears. "The money?" she said.

"Gone. But don't fret. It wasn't much. Most of it's here –" She patted her hidden pocket.

She turned to Nick, who had a split lip but seemed otherwise unhurt. "Let's get out of here," she said, "before there's any more trouble."

They hurried back along the path towards the place where they had come in. Mary Ann was crying now, from shock and fear. They passed several groups of people, but although Jenny looked dishevelled and Nick had a bloody face, no one asked if they needed help. The gardens had become a frightening place. Nick and Jenny hurried her along, and when Nick found the right spot they bundled her quickly through the hedge with its sharp thorns and then out through the gap in the fence onto the towpath.

It was raining harder now, and Mary Ann was cold; her hand hurt and her face and arms smarted from scratches. The few people they passed on the towpath looked either drunk or threatening, and she was glad when they reached the landing stage and found boatmen still plying for hire. What time was it? she wondered. Surely it must be the middle of the night? People were leaving Ranelagh, parties of them coming through the gate, but there were still many more inside.

They climbed into a boat. The boatman looked them over suspiciously and said, "Bit of a scrap, eh?" And

Mary Ann saw, in the light of his lantern, that her dress was muddied all down the front and her hands were dirty and one was bleeding. She whispered to Jenny, "How will I get clean? I can't go to my bed like this…"

Jenny looked at her and frowned, biting her lip. "No. We need to wash those cuts and tidy you up first. Don't worry. We can use the scullery sink."

But she looked shaken, and Mary Ann knew that she was worried.

CHAPTER TWELVE

Gin with Mrs. Bolt

They divided up the takings on the waterfront. Mary Ann's share was more than three guineas. She stowed the coins away in her pocket, and would have felt pleased if she had not been so anxious. It had all gone so well until they were attacked, but now…

They parted from Nick, who slipped away down a narrow street and disappeared. The school was close, but Jenny hesitated. "We need to clean you up, but we could be caught if we do it in the scullery: the noise of water, and the delay... Come to my ma's place. It's just along there, see –" she pointed along the waterfront – "by the Half Moon. We can wash there, and then go back to the school. Safer that way."

Mary Ann followed her obediently. She was relying on Jenny now.

The cottage was tiny – and Jenny's mother only rented the ground floor room. As they approached the door Jenny murmured, "With luck she'll have passed out."

Mary Ann was puzzled by this remark until they went in and she saw a large, dishevelled woman sprawled in a chair by the fireside, breathing heavily. The woman woke with a snort, turned and glared at Jenny.

"What are *you* doing here? Where have you been, dressed like that?"

"I've been to Ranelagh with Nick," Jenny said, in a hard voice that Mary Ann had not heard from her before. "Not that it's any business of yours."

The woman struggled unsteadily to her feet, and her eyes narrowed in her fleshy face. "Who's this you've brought?"

A nearby curtain twitched open a crack, revealing a bed which seemed to contain several children. Two of them began coughing as they woke up. A young voice asked, "Have you brought anything for us, Jenny?"

"Now you've woken the brats," the woman said; and, to the inhabitants of the bed, "Shut that curtain! And your noise!"

Mary Ann felt frightened and out of place. The room was lit by a single tallow candle, which stank of animal fat. Damp laundry hung in every available space: around the fire, on racks from the ceiling. Was it all their own, she wondered, or did Jenny's mother take in washing? On a table was an end of a loaf, and on the floor by the woman's feet an empty bottle – gin, Mary Ann supposed.

A slight sound from the shadows by the hearth

drew her attention. A smaller bed had been placed there, open to the warmth of the fire, and she saw a pale face and tangled brown hair on the pillow.

Jenny dropped to her knees beside the bed. "Dinah, my pet," she said – and her voice now was soft and concerned. "How are you? Poorly?" She looked up. "Ma, have you been giving her that cordial I bought from Mr. Green?"

"Course I did. And made broth, but she won't take it, hardly any. Betty sat with her, spooning it." A watery look came into her eyes. "She's going, Jenny. She's going fast."

"Ssh! She'll hear!" Jenny stroked Dinah's hair. This must be the sister who was ill, Mary Ann realized. "It's all right, Dinah. Jenny's here."

The girl drifted back to sleep.

"She smells," said Jenny, reverting to her hard, accusing voice. "You ought to change her linen."

"Can't do everything, can I?" The woman frowned again at Mary Ann. "Who's she?"

Jenny stood up and put an arm around Mary Ann's shoulders, and drew her forward. "One of the young ladies from the school." And she added sarcastically to Mary Ann: "My mother, Mrs. Bolt."

"What's she doing here?" Mrs. Bolt demanded.

But Jenny ignored her, lit another candle, and took Mary Ann out to a back scullery, where she filled a jug with water from a pail. Part of the main room had been partitioned off with a curtain. Jenny drew the curtain aside and led Mary Ann in. A bed took up most of the space. Next to it was a tiny washstand and a few inches of floor.

"This is *my* space – private," said Jenny. "Any of them comes in here, they get my fist."

Jenny's bed was neat and fresh – a miracle in that house, Mary Ann thought. Her clothes hung on pegs, and the washstand was clean.

She poured water into the bowl. "I'm sorry it's cold, but we can't stop to heat it. Here –" She took a flannel, wetted it and wiped Mary Ann's face, hands and arms in a way that made Mary Ann think she'd done this often, for younger brothers and sisters. The cut hand stung, and blood flowed into the water. Jenny washed it thoroughly, then tore a strip of cloth from something to make a bandage. "You can take that off in the morning. 'Tisn't as bad as it looks. Now, that dress…"

With a dry cloth she brushed at the mud as best she could. "It needs proper cleaning. I'll try and do it with the school wash. Your shoes are not too bad. But your hair…" She took the ribbons out and began combing Mary Ann's hair.

"Ouch!"

"It's all tangled with bits of twig," said Jenny. "Got to get them out. There!" She surveyed Mary Ann. "You don't look so bad now." And as she began to tidy herself, she asked, "Pleased with your money, are you?"

"Yes."

"They liked your singing. I reckon Nick would

be happy to have you with him again!" She put a hand to her pocket. "I'll be able to get some proper medicine for Dinah."

Mary Ann felt troubled. She had never been in a house where people were so poor. Whatever Mrs. Bolt did for a living it seemed that she regularly got drunk and that they all relied on Jenny. It made her own anxiety to continue her singing, deportment and dancing lessons seem frivolous – like icing on a cake: delightful, perhaps, but hardly necessary. These were people who truly needed a few extra guineas. She reached into her own pocket and took out her money, all of it, and held it out to Jenny. "You have it, Jenny. Use it for Dinah, or the other little ones."

"What? Don't be silly." Jenny pushed her hand away.

"But you need it more than I do."

"Keep your money," said Jenny. "You earned it. Come on now. I have to get you home."

Getting back into the school was not as easy as climbing out. Jenny found a flowerpot, and used that to stand on and swing herself up to the sill, where she crouched and slid open the window. The pot scraped against the ground as Mary Ann followed, and they both froze, willing Mrs. Price not to have heard them. Once inside, Mary Ann felt safer. But they had still to creep upstairs in total darkness.

The ground floor was the easiest: only Mrs. Price slept on that floor, and she was on the other side of the house. But on the first floor were the dormitories, one of them close to the back stairs. Mary Ann's heart beat fast every time a stair creaked. But no one stirred, and they set off more confidently for the second floor, feeling their way up. They were almost at the top when Jenny stumbled and slipped down onto the step below with a bump and a muttered curse. Mary Ann thought she would die of fright. Mrs. Corelli's room was next to the stairwell. They waited. Had she heard anything? There was no sound from within.

Now they had reached the landing. Jenny had one more flight to go, up to the attic. Mary Ann had reached her own floor, but she must pass both Mrs. Neave's and Mrs. Corelli's doors before she reached the dormitory.

Jenny gave her a little push. "Go on," she whispered. "I'll wait and make sure you're safe."

They moved apart – and at that moment Mary Ann heard a door open. She gasped as a light appeared in the corridor: a candle, held up in a trembling hand to reveal the startled face of Mrs. Corelli under her nightcap.

"Who…?" she quavered; then, "Mary Ann! Jenny! Whatever is going on?"

CHAPTER THIRTEEN

Caught!

Doors opened all around: Mrs. Neave's, the dormitory; there were even footsteps and voices on the attic landing above.

Then Mrs. Neave emerged, carrying a candle in a holder and wrapped in a dark-coloured robe. Lucy stood blinking and astonished at the end of the corridor.

"Go back to bed, Lucy," said Mrs. Neave. "At once!"

Lucy vanished, pulling the dormitory door shut behind her. Mary Ann longed to be there, safe in the dormitory with Lucy and the others. But she was caught; she could not escape now.

Jenny began to gabble: "Young Miss was taken poorly. I heard her call, and came down. She's better now…" And she edged Mary Ann towards the dormitory, away from the accusing light of the candles.

But Mrs. Neave caught Mary Ann by the shoulder and swung her round. "You have been *outside!*" she said.

Mary Ann knew there was no denying it: her dirty shoes and the mud all down her gown gave her away. Mrs. Neave raised the candle higher and looked at Jenny, who was backing towards the stairs: Jenny with her red dress and white neck and her hat with its jaunty feather. Jenny could hardly pretend she had come down from her bed to attend to a sick girl.

Mrs. Neave's voice was cold: "Go to your room,

Jenny, and report to me first thing in the morning, in my office."

Mary Ann began, "Mrs. Neave, don't blame—"

"As for you, Mary Ann, you will come downstairs now and explain yourself."

Mary Ann reached out wordlessly to Jenny as the maid turned to go. Don't leave me, she wanted to say. She was terrified at the thought of being interrogated alone. But Mrs. Neave gripped her by the shoulders and propelled her towards the stairs. Mary Ann knew from that grip that she was furious.

"I should be grateful if you would come too, Mrs. Corelli," said Mrs. Neave.

As they began to descend Mary Ann heard the dormitory door click open again and voices whispering. Her friends. How she wished she was with them! She felt tears welling up.

She was taken to Mrs. Neave's office. If she had not been so frightened she might have seen the ludicrous side of the situation: the two ladies in nightcaps and wraps facing her as inquisitors in the middle of the night. Mrs. Neave positioned herself behind her desk, but Mrs. Corelli, who had come down barefoot, sat to one side swathed in a lavender-coloured robe and with her hair – or as much of it as was showing – in curl papers. Mary Ann herself was obliged to stand alone in the middle of the floor. Her tears had spilled over on the way downstairs and now great sobs shook her. When Mrs. Neave demanded an explanation she was unable to speak.

"Calm yourself," said Mrs. Neave – to no effect. Her frosty tone only made Mary Ann cry more. Mrs. Corelli suggested, "Perhaps a glass of water...?" and was permitted to fetch one from the decanter on the sideboard.

Mrs. Neave began a bombardment of questions: "Where have you been? Why? What *can* you have been doing? And how did you get so dirty?"

Mary Ann's teeth clunked against the glass and tears rolled down her cheeks as she tried to explain about her plan to raise the money for her school fees.

"*Ranelagh?*" exclaimed Mrs. Neave. "Jenny took you to *Ranelagh* – on a masquerade night? How could the girl possibly afford tickets?"

"We…we broke in. Through a hole in the fence…" Mary Ann saw Mrs. Neave's eyes widening in horror, but she could think of nothing else to tell except the truth. She was forced to explain how they had got out of school through the scullery window, how they had been attacked and robbed, how she had fallen; and all the time she knew she was betraying Jenny, who hadn't wanted to do this at all.

"Please don't blame Jenny!" she said. "I made her do it. I – talked her into it…" She'd been about to say "blackmailed" but that would have meant more betrayal, and she checked herself just in time. "If it wasn't for me," she said, smearing tears across her face with the back of her hand, "Jenny wouldn't have needed to come back here at all. She could have gone home, to her mother's. Sunday's her day off."

"Jenny may be free to go home," said Mrs. Neave coldly, "but she is not free to break out of this house and leave a window unlocked – and especially –" her voice rose – "to take one of my charges with her!" She turned on Mary Ann. "Imagine if something worse had happened to you! If the police had been called? What would I have told your parents? Think of the school's reputation! How many people saw you at Ranelagh?"

"I don't know…a lot…"

"A large number of people who may have guessed where you came from!"

"They only spoke of my singing," said Mary Ann, adding, "Some – several – of them…I don't think they'd remember. They were drunk."

"Drunk!" Mrs. Neave stood up. "And you were there, at night, performing to drunken people…" She turned to Mrs. Corelli: "You know what these masquerade evenings are like. If this becomes known we could be closed down."

Mary Ann began to cry harder than ever. "I'm sorry.

I'm so sorry..." And Mrs. Corelli got up and patted her and gave her a handkerchief and said, "I think Mary Ann should go to bed now, Mrs. Neave."

Mrs. Neave herself seemed suddenly to crumple and look weary. "Yes, indeed, you're right." She turned to Mary Ann and said brusquely, "Dry your eyes, child. At least you've come to no harm. And if you have any money in your pocket you had better give it to me for safekeeping."

Mary Ann untied her pocket and handed it to Mrs. Neave.

She had been crying for so long that she had a lump of pain in her chest that caught at her with every breath. "I wanted – I only wanted – to earn some money," she said, the words coming out in gasps. "Eight guineas. For next term. I don't want to leave."

The two teachers exchanged a glance, and Mrs. Neave said, more kindly, "I understand. But it is not in your power to raise that money, Mary Ann. Nor in mine. Now go to bed. You may sleep in the sick room tonight. I don't want you disturbing the other girls. Mrs. Corelli will take you up."

The sick room was an annexe attached to Mrs. Neave's suite of rooms by a connecting door. It contained a narrow bed and a washstand and looked, Mary Ann thought, like a prison cell.

Mrs. Corelli saw her look, and seemed to guess what she was thinking. She gave Mary Ann a hug. "Don't worry. It won't seem so bad in the morning. Go to sleep now."

She shut the door, and Mary Ann lay down alone in the little room and cried with her fist pushed hard against her mouth. It wasn't only her own disgrace that distressed her; it was knowing that she'd brought trouble on Jenny. She couldn't forgive herself for that.

Soon she heard the first birds chirping outside. There was a pale, cold light in the room.

I'll never sleep, she thought. But she did.

She woke late. There was no sound from the other side of the connecting door. She got out of bed and, still in her chemise, cautiously opened the door to the corridor. Smells and sounds of breakfast rose from below: a distant clatter of cutlery, a hum of voices.

Breakfast. That meant it was at least half past seven. The maids would have been up for hours. And Mrs. Neave had told Jenny to report to her first thing.

With a sense of foreboding, Mary Ann darted barefoot out of the room and upstairs to the attic.

"Jenny...?"

She'd never been up here before and didn't know which room Jenny slept in. She pushed tentatively at a door. It opened to reveal a long, low-ceilinged room containing three beds. Two were made up. One had been stripped.

"Jenny!"

She ran out, and collided with a maid coming in: Ellen, the kitchen maid, a skinny girl with a hunted expression – always in trouble.

"Oh, Miss! You scared me!" She looked hangdog. "Been sent to change my apron."

The apron was filthy with hand-wipings. Mary Ann shuddered. "Where's Jenny?" she asked. "Is she downstairs?"

"She's gone!" The girl's eyes lit up at the prospect of gossip.

"Gone?"

"Yes! Got her wages, packed, and left. Been dismissed!"

"But she can't –"

Mary Ann ran to the dormitory, found clean clothes, dressed, and raced downstairs. She arrived in the front hall as everyone was coming out of the dining room. Mrs. Neave, carrying some books, was shepherding a group of older girls towards the front classroom. Mary Ann burst into their midst and confronted the teacher.

"Mrs. Neave! It wasn't Jenny's fault! Let her come back – please!"

Mrs. Neave paused, and Mary Ann quailed at her expression.

The girls watched with obvious interest. Mrs. Neave waved them towards the classroom. "Go and sit down and begin reading Chapter Two."

She drew Mary Ann away from the busy hall, into her office.

"*Never* run and shout like that in public, Mary Ann," she said.

"But, Mrs. Neave, why did you dismiss Jenny?" Mary Ann felt overwhelmed with guilt.

"I should have thought that was obvious. She is untrustworthy, dishonest, and quite unfit to work in an establishment such as this."

"But it was *me*! *My* fault!" Mary Ann twisted her hands together and struggled not to cry.

"Jenny is an adult, Mary Ann. You were certainly at fault, but you must not blame yourself for what has happened to her."

"But she won't be able to get another place!" She

knew Jenny must have left without a reference.

"That is not my concern," said Mrs. Neave. And she added, "I've had my eye on Jenny Bolt for some time."

Mary Ann wondered what she meant; whether it was something to do with the pillowcases. Perhaps Jenny *had* taken them.

"Her sister is ill – dying," she said. "And her mother drinks, and Jenny buys medicine for Dinah and looks after them all. I know. I went to their house. If she…if she *took* anything it would have been for her sister."

Mrs. Neave sighed. "I know she was your friend, Mary Ann, and your concern does you credit, but believe me, I was obliged to dismiss her. Go off to your class now. Arithmetic, isn't it? I'm afraid you have missed breakfast. If you feel hungry perhaps it will remind you to be more careful of your behaviour in future. And I must consider what your punishment is to be. We'll speak later this morning."

In the garden, during the break after lunch, Sophia, Lucy and Phoebe clustered round and clamoured to know everything. They were astonished at Mary Ann's adventures and hugely impressed by her account of how much she had earned.

"You *sang* at Ranelagh and earned all that!" exclaimed Sophia. "And you never told us what you were going to do! You *toad*!" she added, affectionately.

"I wish we'd known!" said Lucy.

"You'd have been in trouble, then, like me." Mary Ann bit her lip. "And Jenny."

"Oh! About Jenny…" Phoebe looked important: the bearer of news. They all turned to her. "Charlotte Cross told me she overheard Mrs. Price and Cook talking about Jenny. They said she'd been stealing: things had been disappearing from the linen room for months."

"*Months?*"

So that was what Mrs. Neave had been hinting at. Was it true? And what things? They couldn't all have been for Dinah, surely? Mary Ann's trust in Jenny began to waver. And yet Jenny had been kind to her, and honest; she couldn't believe she was no more than a common thief. And even if she was, did that make it right for Mary Ann to betray her?

Her confusion over Jenny was bewildering. But at least the other girls were full of sympathy for *her*. On Mrs. Neave's orders Mary Ann was confined to the house for the rest of term, obliged to read and copy out improving texts, and banned from the garden and from taking part in Saturday outings. Only church on Sundays was permitted. She was quite a heroine, however – escaping from robbers, admired by the grand people at Ranelagh. And the school still had her earnings. Perhaps, Mary Ann thought, when her punishment was over, Mrs. Neave would allow her to stay another half a term for three and a half guineas?

Lucy brought her back to earth. "Will Mrs. Neave tell your parents?"

"I don't know." She had thought of this, but hadn't

dared ask. Her parents would be so angry if they found out. They would probably beat her.

Lucy pondered her own question. "I don't think she will. I don't think she would want them to know that you had been so badly supervised."

That was a cheering thought – and probably true, Mary Ann thought.

But next morning, during French Conversation, Mrs. Price called for Mary Ann and said that she was wanted in the office.

"You have visitors," she said.

CHAPTER FOURTEEN

Mary Ann on Trial

Mary Ann knocked timidly on Mrs. Neave's door.

Visitors, Mrs. Price had said. It could only be her parents, summoned by Mrs. Neave, come to chastise and humiliate her. Even worse, they would be angry with Mrs. Neave, as Lucy had said. Suppose there was an argument? Her father would be sure to shout. I shan't be able to bear it, she thought, if my father makes a fuss and people hear.

"Come in," said Mrs. Neave.

Two women sat in the visitors' chairs. One was Mary Ann's mother. For a moment Mary Ann did not recognize the sharp-faced older woman wearing an elegant but slightly old-fashioned hat. Then she exclaimed, "Grandmama!" and dropped a curtsy. Her mind was racing. Why was her grandmother here? Was the whole family to be involved in her disgrace? It would be too dreadful to bear.

She was surprised when her grandmother looked her up and down with evident approval.

"You've grown," she said.

People always said that. But Mary Ann realized that her grandmother had not seen her for…how long was it? Two years? Three? Mrs. Causey looked much the same, but Mary Ann realized that she herself must have changed greatly.

Mrs. Causey stood up. "Let me look at you. Walk over there." She turned to Mrs. Neave. "Well, she is quite the young lady! Is this your work, Mrs. Neave?"

"We encourage good deportment and manners," said Mrs. Neave, smiling benignly at Mary Ann.

"Mary Ann is very happy here," added her mother, also with a fond glance.

Mary Ann was bewildered. This was not at all what she had expected. Why was everyone so amiable? Had Mrs. Neave not told them, after all? Was she about to do so?

Mary Ann composed her face into a mask of demure submission – suitable, she hoped, for whatever might come next.

"The child's happiness is not essential," said Mrs. Causey, in response to her daughter – and Mary Ann tensed – "but nevertheless I am glad to hear it. Do you work hard, Mary Ann?"

This remark, addressed suddenly to her, startled Mary Ann. "Yes!" she said breathlessly. "Yes, of course, Grandmama."

"No 'of course' about it," retorted her grandmother. "Your mother was as idle as a cat at your age."

"Mama!" protested Mary Ann's mother.

Mary Ann gazed at the floorboards and Mrs. Neave intervened smoothly, "We are all very pleased with Mary Ann. She works hard at her lessons, and is particularly gifted at music."

"Ah, yes, the music!" said Mrs. Causey. "I must hear you sing, Mary Ann."

Mary Ann experienced a moment of panic: here? Now? But it seemed not, for Mrs. Neave said, "Mrs. Causey, I suggest that I take you and Mrs. Giffard on a tour of the school, and show you Mary Ann's work books. And I'm sure Mrs. Corelli would be delighted to play the harpsichord to accompany her singing. Would you like to take tea first?"

They agreed. Mrs. Neave rang for the maid and ordered tea, then asked them to excuse her while she went to speak to the teachers. Mary Ann was left alone with her mother and grandmother. She looked cautiously from one to another of them. Did they know? If they didn't, she was not going to tell them.

"You must be surprised to see us here together," her mother began. Her voice sounded strained. "As you know, I have never liked to ask for help—"

"But common sense has at last prevailed," interrupted Mrs. Causey. "Your mother wrote and told me of your father's financial incompetence and asked me for help with your school fees."

As they spoke Mary Ann felt her anxiety dropping away and her spirits lifting. This was nothing to do with the Ranelagh episode. Her grandmother was going to pay for her to stay on at school!

"Of course, before I could agree to do so," her grandmother continued, "I wanted to see your school and your work, which is why we are here. I need to know that my investment in you will be worthwhile."

At this moment the tea arrived, followed by Mrs. Neave carrying a pile of school books and some drawings that Mary Ann had done in her art class.

Mary Ann shrank with embarrassment and a fear that her work would not be considered good enough.

But Mrs. Neave, all charm and confidence, evidently had no such worries as she showed her pupil's work.

While her grandmother looked through the books and murmured approval, Mary Ann glanced gratefully at her mother. She knew what it must have cost her to ask for help from Grandmama. Although her mother never spoke against their grandmother, Harriet had told Mary Ann that Grandmama disapproved not only of their father but of almost every other choice their mother had made.

Mrs. Giffard sat quietly now, letting Mrs. Causey do the talking, and scarcely taking part in the discussion about Mary Ann's work. She was not at all her usual self; she always dwindled in her mother's presence. Mary Ann remembered, with a pang of guilt, how she had thought that her mother didn't care about her, only about Harriet. It wasn't true. She almost reached out and took her mother's hand – but that would have been too embarrassing in public. Instead she gave a small smile, and her mother responded in the same way.

When Mrs. Causey had declared herself satisfied with Mary Ann's schoolwork and drawing ("adequate" was how she described her granddaughter's sketching ability) they all went upstairs to the music room, where Mrs. Corelli was waiting for them. Nervously, Mary Ann played one of the harpsichord pieces Mr. Ashton had taught her; and then Mrs. Corelli put "When Daisies Pied and Violets Blue" on the music stand, and Mary Ann sang to her accompaniment. Her voice, when she began, was tremulous. Not only was she anxious to impress but she had done a lot of crying in the last day or so and felt quite hoarse. But Mrs. Corelli caught her eye and smiled encouragingly, and soon she was singing with confidence.

As she finished with the chorus of "cuckoos" – one after another sung by her and echoed by the harpsichord – she saw her grandmother smile. Mrs. Neave smiled too and said, "Mary Ann will sing that song, and others, I believe, at our concert in September. She is one of our most gifted singers. We are delighted to have her in the choir."

Mrs. Causey looked pleased, and Mrs. Neave, encouraged, went on, "We take the girls to a concert at Ranelagh every year, where they can hear the very best musicians and singers and observe genteel behaviour. This year we were fortunate enough to see the Mozart children perform."

"Oh, Grandmama, it was such a wonderful occasion!" Mary Ann broke in without thinking. "I do so long to perform like Miss Mozart!"

Mrs. Causey's expression changed. "I hope you do not think of performing in public, Mary Ann?"

"Oh! No – of course not…" Mary Ann lowered her eyes modestly and was silent.

"It is not necessary, or even desirable, for a lady to excel," said her grandmother. "Tell me, Mary Ann, what *do* you consider to be the purpose of your education here?"

Mary Ann knew she had to give the right answer.

Her fate might depend upon it.

"To acquire ladylike accomplishments and learn how to converse and behave in society."

"To what end?"

"To make a good marriage."

"Indeed." Her grandmother scrutinized Mary Ann's face, as if suspecting her of wanting more. Then she turned to her daughter. "Well, Susan, I have no wish to see my granddaughter disadvantaged by her father's folly. I shall be pleased to pay for her education at Mrs. Neave's school for as long as necessary."

"Oh!" Mary Ann thought she had never felt so happy. There were smiles and thanks all round, and even as she stammered out her own genuine gratitude she saw how her grandmother relished this moment of power.

"Let me make clear," Mrs. Causey said sternly, "that there must be no talk of performing on the stage – nowhere more public than the school concert or a friend's drawing room. Your singing is intended to be an ornament, Mary Ann, not a calling. Do you understand?"

"Yes, Grandmama," said Mary Ann.

All her friends were delighted with Mary Ann's news. That evening, as they sat and chatted in the dormitory, Mary Ann pulled out the charity concert ticket from its hiding place in the panelling, and gazed at the picture. She still loved Ranelagh, in spite of her last experience. She thought of those singers in their silk gowns and powdered hair, and of Maria Anna Mozart. One day, she thought, I'll sing there, in the Rotunda. I'll be on that stage, under those glittering chandeliers, and the applause will be for me.

"Lights out, girls!" called Mrs. Corelli.

Mary Ann pushed the ticket back into its place – but this time it slipped right inside, out of reach! She picked at the edge of it with her fingernail, but only succeeded in pushing it further in. She hunted for a hairpin.

"What's the matter?" asked Sophia.

"My Ranelagh ticket. It's gone into the panelling."

Sophia produced tweezers, but it was no good. She had lost it. The ticket was visible, but quite out of reach.

Like my ambition to sing at the opera, thought Mary Ann. Perhaps one day…but for now she knew she must keep her dreams secret.

CHAPTER FIFTEEN

Many Voices

Dear Sis, wrote George, *What excellent news! Fancy the old girl coming up with the money like that! I wonder how long she and Mama will stay friends? She is quite a dragon, I recall (better burn this after reading). Papa must be furious. I wish I'd been at home when Mama told him what she'd done! I suppose by the time he found out, it was too late to prevent it. He never mentioned it to me in his last letter, but it seems he has become involved in* another likely venture, so his mind will be on that. Perhaps this time he will make our fortunes, and then Hatty can find another suitor and spurn the odious Mr. Browne.

What is this escapade of yours that you hint at? Is it really so dreadful that you can only whisper the details to me when next we meet? Surely not?

Alas, dear Sis, much as I'd love to hear you sing, I shall be in the midst of examinations on that date. Greek and Latin call. Be good – and remember me to Grandmama.

Your loving brother,

George

Dear George, wrote Mary Ann. Really you should not be so rude about Grandmama. I believe that at heart she is kind, and probably also rather lonely. As she lives nearby, in Kensington, she has promised to call occasionally on a Saturday and take me out. I shall introduce her to the Bun House; and she says she may take me to see the royal tombs in Westminster Abbey.

Harriet writes with good news. Her friend Elizabeth

Dunn is travelling with an aunt to Paris, where they will stay for six weeks, and Harriet is invited to go with them! She is hugely excited and glad to be away from all the gossip about her and Mr. Browne. She says she would not have Mr. Browne now if he were to beg her on bended knee.

I should be jealous of Harriet's good fortune were I not so happy here. We are busy practising for our concert, and we also go outside often in the fine weather. And, George, you will never guess! The Mozart family are staying here, in Chelsea — quite near us, in Five Fields Row — and Sophia and I saw them in the street while we were out walking: Mrs. Mozart, that is, and Wolfgang and Nannerl! We were so very delighted! I am much taken with Nannerl's looks. She is of a height similar to mine, and fair, like me, but much prettier. I am trying to do my hair in the same style as hers; Sophia helps me. Mrs. Corelli heard that Mr. Mozart has been ill and so they have taken lodgings here because the air is fresher than in London; but they have given no concerts for several weeks and none is planned till he recovers. Mrs. Corelli says it is a chancy profession. I think she intended that remark as a warning to me.

Mary Ann paused, and put down her pen. She had also seen someone else she knew that day, while walking back to the school. It had been market day, and the voices of the fruit, vegetable and flower sellers competed with each other in a tangle of sing-song calls:

"Buy my sweet lavender!"

"Plums! Juicy plums! Fresh picked today!"

"A rose, sir? A red rose for your sweetheart?"

And then Mary Ann had heard another voice – one she knew well: "Apples! Ripe red apples! First of the season!"

It was Jenny. She stood behind a stall piled high with fruit, singing out her wares in that clear, musical voice that Mary Ann remembered. She was a queen among the stallholders: tall, dark-eyed, fine-looking even in her simple dress and coarse apron. There was an older woman on the same stall; not her mother –

her employer, Mary Ann supposed. Jenny was clearly good for trade with her voice and good looks. She saw Mary Ann, caught her eye, and smiled, widening her eyes in surprise.

Mary Ann approached the stall.

"You're still at school, then, Miss?" Jenny said.

"Oh, yes! My grandmother –"

But it was impossible to talk. Jenny turned away to serve a customer, filling a bag with apples.

"I'm sorry," Mary Ann said, when Jenny turned back to her. "I tried to tell Mrs. Neave…"

Jenny shrugged. "I prefer the market – not so many rules! And I wait tables at the Duke of York and sing there some evenings. All I want now is better lodgings. Yes, sir? Can I help you?"

She smiled and moved away, and Mary Ann left and returned to her friends. She felt great relief. Jenny didn't blame her for what had happened. And she had found work, despite not being given a reference by Mrs. Neave. Mary Ann didn't care what others said about Jenny;

Jenny had been a good friend to her, whatever else she'd done. She, Mary Ann, was the one who had let her friend down and caused her to be dismissed…

She continued her letter to George: *The programme for our concert will be printed tomorrow. I am to be on first, after the choir have sung "Nymphs and Shepherds". Think of me before you go in to your examination — and I'll think of you.*
With love, your sister,
Mary Ann

"I need the privy again," said Sophia.

It was the day of the concert, and the girls were in the dormitory, making sure they had handkerchiefs and fans, that there were no holes in their stockings, no scuff marks on their silk slippers. The privies were two flights down, in the back yard. They had all been queuing there earlier, for a long time.

"It's only nerves," said Lucy. "You can't join that queue again."

She and Phoebe were more relaxed, as they merely had their work on show and were not performing.

"The audience are starting to arrive," said Phoebe. She led them out to look down through the central drop in the stairwell to a narrow segment of chequered hall floor far below. No visitors were visible, but Mary Ann could hear their voices: a hum of pleased anticipation.

"We'll be called down soon," said Phoebe.

Sophia clutched herself. "I *have* to go again!"

"Use the pot," said Mary Ann. "We'll wait out here."

Sophia darted into the dormitory.

Mary Ann felt the same mixture of nervousness and excitement. I wonder if professional performers feel like this, she thought; or do they get used to it?

Earlier that day they had seen the two downstairs front rooms transformed for the occasion. The dining room was full of tables draped in white linen on which were displayed the best examples of the girls' work in writing, French composition, sewing, drawing and painting. Across the hall, the front classroom had been cleared of its globe, wall displays and desks, and set out with chairs for both audience and performers. The harpsichord from the dining room had been brought in and placed near the window. Both rooms were full of flowers, and the smell of roses, mingled with the visitors' perfumes, floated up the stairwell.

The girls all wore pale summer gowns, and Mary Ann and her friends had arranged each other's hair. Mary Ann hoped hers looked like Nannerl Mozart's. Mrs. Corelli had briefly inspected them all earlier and given her approval.

Sophia came back. They looked down the stairwell, but saw only the heads of other girls also looking down. The sounds from below were fainter now. The audience must all be seated. Mary Ann felt light-headed with nerves.

Then came the sound of Mr. Ashton playing the harpsichord. That was their signal. Mrs. Corelli appeared on the stairs, and they followed her down and joined the girls from the first floor. They all filed into the concert room to take their places, either with the choir or along the sides of the room.

Mary Ann, Sophia, and the other soloists sat in the front row of the choir. Sophia gripped Mary Ann's hand. "I shall faint!" she whispered melodramatically.

Mrs. Neave stood up to speak to the audience. Mary Ann heard scarcely anything of what she said; she was too nervous and too busy scanning the audience for her family. Heads, hats, feathers, flickering fans… *There* they were, in the centre: Mama, Grandmama, Harriet – and Papa! She was surprised to see her father – especially with Grandmama, whom she knew he disliked. Perhaps Mama had talked him into coming. Dear Mama, she thought, she has been so kind to me; she must have hated going to Grandmama for help. And yet the two of them were chatting and smiling together now, and even Papa appeared to be at his most amiable. She caught her sister's eye and gave a little wave, and Harriet waved back.

And then Mrs. Neave finished talking, and moved to one side, and Mr. Ashton began to play. The choir stood up to the introduction to "Nymphs and Shepherds".

Singing with the choir calmed Mary Ann's nerves; there was safety in the mingled voices:

"*Nymphs and shepherds, come away,*

Come away…"

When the song was over the audience applauded warmly, with smiles and cheers; and a plump, magnificently red-haired lady who could only be Sophia's mother, called out, "Bravo!"

Then the clapping died away, and Mrs. Corelli nodded to Mary Ann, who stood up and walked out in front. From the harpsichord came the introduction to Galatea's air. Mary Ann sang:

"*As when the dove*

Laments her love,

All on the naked spray;
When he returns,
No more she mourns,
But love the live-long day…"

She heard the notes in her head, and they came out as she heard them: perfect. She relaxed, and forgot her nerves, and sang for the joy of it.

When she sat down, and the applause began, she thought: I shall always have this. Even if I don't sing at Covent Garden, don't become famous; no matter what happens to me I shall have the music and it will always make me happy.

But she would not give up her dreams – not yet.

She looked out at her family and smiled.

Author's Note

Mary Ann's story will take you back to 1764 – a time when Chelsea was a village on the outskirts of London. At that date Number Six, Chelsea Walk, was closer to the river because the Embankment had not yet been built.

Visitors were drawn to Chelsea by the popularity of Ranelagh Gardens. The concert in this story really did take place, and the young Wolfgang Amadeus Mozart was one of the performers. In 1764 Mozart and his sister Nannerl were performing regularly together in London. I can find no proof that Nannerl was also at Ranelagh that day, but as the two children usually appeared together it seems likely that she was. Their father promoted his children as prodigies and in his advertisements he actually knocked a year off each child's age to make them seem even more amazing. In this story they are given their real ages. Nannerl Mozart was a brilliant musician who was gradually overshadowed by the genius of her younger brother.

The songs Mary Ann sings were all popular at the time, and are still sung. I used to sing some of them in my school choir in the 1950s!

I hope you will enjoy reading this story and meeting another of the girls who have lived at 6 Chelsea Walk.

Ann Turnbull

ABOUT THE AUTHOR

Ann Turnbull knew from an early age that she wanted to be a writer. After working as a secretary for many years, Ann returned to studying and started to train as a teacher. It was then that she rediscovered children's literature and began writing for children herself. Her first novel was published in 1974 and she is now a full-time author. She has written more than thirty books for children and young adults, including *Pigeon Summer*, which was shortlisted for the Nestlé Smarties Book Prize, and *No Shame, No Fear*, shortlisted for the Guardian Children's Fiction prize and the Whitbread Children's Book Award.

Ann lives with her husband in Shropshire.

To find out more about Ann Turnbull, you can visit her website: www.annturnbull.com.

Discover more inspirational stories from
6 Chelsea Walk, and the girls who lived there
throughout history...

Girls for the Vote
1914
LINDA NEWBERY

When Polly discovers her new neighbours are suffragettes,
fighting for women's right to vote, she is determined to join
their protest march. But her parents are scandalized. Will she
dare to defy them and do what she thinks is right?

Girls with a Voice
1764
ANN TURNBULL

Mary Ann's greatest wish is to become an opera singer, but
when she is told she must leave her boarding school, her singing
dreams are shattered. Distraught, she comes up with a plan to
stay at school, oblivious to the danger it will put her in...

Coming soon...

Girls Behind the Camera
1895
ADÈLE GERAS

Cecily is enchanted when she meets Rosalind, a photographer,
who seems to be the perfect match for Cecily's lonely
widowed father. But her father's friend, the dull Miss
Braithwaite, keeps spoiling her plans to unite the pair. Will
Cecily's dreams ever come true?

Girls with Courage
1857
ADÈLE GERAS

When Lizzie's stepfather sends her to stay with relatives in London, Lizzie struggles to adapt to her new life of stiff manners and formal pastimes. She lives for the daily letters from her mother, but when the letters suddenly stop, Lizzie sets out to discover the truth and finds herself on a rescue mission.

Girls on the Up
1969
LINDA NEWBERY

Andie dreams of becoming an artist and loves living in Chelsea, with the fashion, music and art galleries along the trendy King's Road. There's even a real artist living in the flat downstairs. Could Andie's paintings, inspired by the excitement of the first-ever moon landing, be good enough for her to achieve her dreams?

Girls at War
1941
ANN TURNBULL

When Josie goes to stay with her cousin, Edith, during the Blitz, she tries to fit in by joining Edith and her friends in teasing a timid classmate. But when the bullying gets out of hand, Josie faces a dilemma: she knows what it feels like to be picked on, but if she takes a stand, will Edith tell everyone her secret?

USBORNE QUICKLINKS

For links to websites where you can listen to music from Mary Ann's time and find out more about the Mozart children and Ranelagh Gardens, go to the Usborne Quicklinks website at www.usborne.com/quicklinks and type in the title of this book.

At Usborne Quicklinks you can:

- Listen to songs Mary Ann loved to sing
- Watch a musician play a harpsichord and find out how it works
- See some of the fashions of the day
- Find out more about everyday life in the 1700s

Please follow the online safety guidelines at the Usborne Quicklinks website.